THORNS AMONG SHADOWS:

A RAPUNZEL RETELLING

BY ALLY KELLY

Copyright © 2024 by Ally Kelly

All rights reserved.

No part of this book may be reproduced in any form or by any electronic or mechanical means, including information storage and retrieval systems, without written permission from the author, except for the use of brief quotations in a book review.

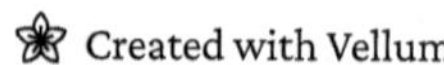 Created with Vellum

*For Harrison and Emmie -
may you always chase after your dreams*

CHAPTER ONE

Meira's arm felt heavy as her fingers traced the letters etched into the cold, smooth stone marking her sister Eirian's grave. It sat at the back of the garden beneath a large oak tree. Their mother's gravestone stood next to it, covered in moss and its letters beginning to fade, while Eirian's was fresher, only six months old.

Six months.

The sickness, though lasting only months, had felt like a lifetime. Father had fallen sick first but managed to recover without lingering effects. Eirian though. . . Eirian succumbed after months of fighting. And her death rattled Meira's father to his core, his grief weakening his heart.

Meira took a shuddering breath as a late summer breeze, unusually chill for the season, blew through the garden. She looked over her shoulder, at the lone swing hanging from the oak's branch slowly swaying in the breeze, and thought back to the times she and her sister had spent pushing each other on it—such a simpler time.

While looking back at the gravestones, Meira placed a hand on top of Eirian's. She stood, turning to see her father,

Lord Daesyn, in an emerald-green cloak. His beard was freshly shaved, his short-trimmed hair a mix of salt and pepper. At first glance, he was as she'd always known him —tall, handsome, and blue eyed, with a great mind for literature and storytelling. The ornate cane he steadied himself with served as a cold reminder of their tragedy.

"Meira, it's cold out," he said, his voice gentle. "You aren't dressed for the weather."

Meira looked down at her clothes—a green, short-sleeved tunic and a long riding skirt with brown boots, paired with matching bracers. Her quiver of arrows and bow tucked in its sheath rested against the trunk of the tree. Her long, curly red hair sat braided on her shoulder. She'd gone riding through the forest early that morning, taking her horse, Vala, down the path leading to the waterfall she and Eirian would often play at when they were young.

Meira had been out in much chillier temperatures than this, and normally she would say he was worrying for nothing, but the cold air had been what led to his and Eirian's sickness, so she couldn't blame him. The city physician had been to see him when he'd first taken ill and said it should be gone within a few weeks. When he still hadn't improved month later, and it had only gotten worse, the court physician was called next, thanks to his status as a council member. Her father finally recovered after a few more weeks, but his health hadn't been quite the same.

Meira gave her father a gentle smile, walking to his side. "I know, Father. I'm sorry. I let myself fall into my thoughts."

A yawning silence fell between them as their gazes wandered toward the gravestones. After a moment, her father cleared his throat. "The carriage bringing us to the capital will be ready to take us soon," he said.

Meira hid her scowl with effort. Her father knew well just how much Meira despised the idea of going to court for the whole spring season, possibly through the summer as well, but she didn't want to make him feel any more guilty than he likely did. After all, Eirian had been the eldest daughter. Eirian was the one who was to take his place at court. She'd had the mind for it, the social savvy to navigate politics, and a knack for sifting useful information from gossip. Being surrounded by boring gossip at court wasn't something Meira had ever seen in her future, but it seemed fate had other plans in mind.

Though her father's mind was still sharp, the Ivory Council had expressed concern that his age, paired with his weakened heart, may inhibit his ability to travel between court and his estate and had proposed training a replacement to take his place. Since Eirian had passed, that left Meira, who felt forced to take both their places for fear of losing their status at court and, ultimately, their family home. She couldn't allow that to happen.

Court in the kingdom of Alythia met annually in the spring, which meant being there for two or three months, depending on how the council sessions went. The Daesyn family owned two estates—a smaller house in the capital city, for the convenience of going back and forth to court, and their true home, located at the edge of the kingdom, where she and Eirian had been born.

Meira and her father would ride to the capital city, then Meira would begin her journey into court life. She couldn't help but feel resentful toward her sister. Meira wanted to, instead, stay in the countryside, riding her horse through the forest and practicing archery in peace. But wants were not reality.

The transition to the capital would take a few days. They'd have to stop to water and feed the horses and would stay at a small inn along the way. They'd reach the estate within the city by the following afternoon, and by the third day, Meira would continue on to the castle.

Meira's father placed a hand on her arm, gently pulling her toward the garden entrance. She allowed him to lead her, taking one last glance back at the gravestones.

* * *

Meira watched out the carriage window as they rode farther and farther away from her childhood home. She'd been to the capital city a scant number of times, and the castle itself even less, and knew she'd feel out of place there. Her usual activities would be curtailed, including ones that weren't considered especially ladylike. Instead, she'd be expected to sit in the throne room when the royal family—Prince Gaelen and the Queen Regent, Queen Averith—were there, and otherwise sit in on most council meetings. Her hands twisted into sweaty knots at the thought.

Meira shifted to lean out the window, looking back toward the house as the carriage moved farther along the main road. She swallowed hard, blinking back the tears threatening her eyes as she silently said goodbye to her childhood home. Who knew how long it would be before she returned, or how much she'd have changed in that time? She heaved a frustrated sigh and turned back in her seat, directing her gaze forward out the window.

Meira thought back to the last time she'd seen Prince

Gaelen. Her father had to come to the castle for a special council meeting and brought Meira and Eirian with him. Eirian had gone off with their cousin Haelyn, but Meira explored the castle, only to end up lost. She'd entered the library, where she found Prince Gaelen sitting on the floor with a pile of books next to him.

Meira smiled at the memory. It seemed like such a lifetime ago now. She'd apologized for disturbing the prince, but a spark had appeared in his blue eyes, and Gaelen invited her to sit with him. She'd hesitated, but his smirk intrigued her, and so she ultimately joined him, talking about books and the stories her father had told her. They spent the whole day together, wandering the castle. Gaelen showed her some of the hidden passageways, leading all the way down into the depths of the castle where ancient royal family heirlooms were kept.

By the end of the day, they'd made their way out into the courtyard, where Gaelen showed her how to shoot a bow and arrow. It was later that day, when they'd gone back to their home in the city, that Meira begged her father to finally teach her archery. Traditionally, the art of archery had been passed down in their family for a few generations now, and her father was glad to see that she, at least, was eager to learn the skill. From that day forward, she had worked diligently and even began teaching herself to shoot a target while riding Vala.

The one upside to returning to court after all this time would be seeing Prince Gaelen again. She wondered how much he'd changed in the seven years that had passed, and whether he would even remember her, or the time they'd spent together.

Seeming to sense Meira's frustration, her father looked up from the parchment sprawled in his lap, placing it down next to him on the seat. Reaching a hand across, he took one of her hands in his, giving it a gentle squeeze.

"We'll be passing the oasis soon," he said. "It's supposedly the location of the fairy-blessed well that helps to keep the crops growing. Some of the villagers say that just a sprinkle of its water keeps them growing, even during a drought."

Meira always enjoyed when her father told her stories —it helped make the time go by faster, especially on long journeys.

* * *

Late in the afternoon of their second day of travel, the carriage arrived at the bottom of a long cobblestone path winding its way into the capital city. The carriage jerked to an abrupt halt, nearly throwing Meira into her father's lap. She frowned and curiously poked her head out the window. To the right, a city guard stood by the carriage coachman, his silver cloak flowing in the soft wind. Meira strained to hear the conversation, but the guard glanced in her direction, giving her a hard look before turning his back to her.

"Don't worry, we won't be here for long," her father said. "It's just a routine inspection. They always do this when the court is about to be in session."

"What are they checking for?" Meira asked.

"Unauthorized weapons, usually," her father replied.

Meira frowned, trying to remember the last time she'd visited the capital. "Is it normal for them to check for weapons? What about my bow and arrows?"

Lord Daesyn heaved a sigh. "They've been a bit stricter about it since the death of King Torryn," he replied. "Don't worry about your bow. I've already made sure the coachman notifies the guards that you've been pre-autho-rized to have it."

Things in Alythia had changed since King Torryn's death. It was as though a shadow had hung itself over the kingdom—stricter laws, villagers struggling to keep food on their tables due to higher taxes. Even Meira's father had mentioned the council meetings being harder to sit through.

Meira thought back to the day she'd learned of King Torryn's death. She'd gone looking for her father, finding both the study and sitting room empty. She made her way outside and into the garden, walking along the path, and found him sitting on a bench along the stone path. A piece of parchment was clutched tight in his hand, his head down.

Pulling her cloak around her, Meira had walked over to him and knelt in front of him, placing a gentle hand on his knee.

"Father, what is it?" she asked.

Sadness she'd not seen since her mother's death filled his eyes as he looked up at her. "King Torryn has died."

Meira held in a gasp, moving to sit down on the bench. Her father and Torryn had been friends for many years, since they were both young. Meira knew how much the king and his friendship had meant to her father. Wrapping her arms around him gently, she sat with him in silence until he was finally ready to head inside. As they sat, Meira thought of Prince Gaelen and what the king's death would mean for him.

After a moment, the carriage jolted forward again, beginning its way up the winding road. They soon came to another stop, this time at the house. The coachman opened the door and put a hand out for Meira. Meira placed her hand in his and stepped out of the carriage, staring up at the house.

Meira's father climbed out of the carriage and stood next to her, placing a hand on her arm as he adjusted his hold on his walking stick. "Come, Meira. We'll unpack and get settled in," he said.

As she walked toward the house, she caught sight of the family emblem and motto painted on its side. The emblem was that of a sprig of juniper, crossed with an arrow, with the words *strong of root, strong of thorn* written below. The Daesyn family had received a noble title for their archery skills many years ago during the War of Ivory. Being able to carry on those skills was something Meira always prided herself on.

Meira followed her father into the house, finding herself standing in the foyer. To her right was a sitting room with a fireplace and bookshelves lined with rows of books. To her left was the staircase leading upstairs to the bedrooms.

The bedroom she'd shared with Eirian was at the end of the hall, its door shut. Echoes of her and Eirian's giggles rang in her ears. As she climbed the spiral staircase, she realized she hadn't been back to the capital estate since before Eirian's death.

Meira came to the end of the hallway, staring at the door for a moment before placing her hand on the door-knob and opening the door. The musty odor of dust entered her nostrils, forcing her to sneeze as she entered the room. Two beds sat to her left, one each tucked in opposite corners, with a small dresser and candlestick sitting between them.

Meira walked to the desk sitting straight ahead, where a strew of parchment and a book lay. Hot tears pricked at her eyes, and she forcibly blinked them back as she thought back to the last time she'd been in this room with her sister, before her sickness became too much for her. Their father had wanted Eirian to stay closer to the capital, but Eirian insisted on returning to their country home, where it was more peaceful and she could be laid to rest with their mother.

Meira shook her head, reaching up to rub her eyes.

"I miss you, Eirian," she whispered.

"Meira?"

Meira's father leaned against the doorframe, a soft smile on his lips. "I was wondering where you'd gone off to," he said. "Dinner will be ready shortly, and then perhaps we can take a short walk through the city. There's a book-shop nearby I thought you might want to visit."

Meira smiled, walking over to her father, standing on her tiptoes to kiss him on the cheek. "I'd like that very much, Father. I'll get changed and be down shortly."

* * *

That night, Meira sat on the floor in front of the fireplace, watching the flames dance. Her father sat in his chair a few feet away, a book sprawled open on his lap as he read, fire-light reflecting off his spectacles against the contrast of shadowplay on the wall. Meira had explored the grounds after they'd unpacked and gone to the bookshop but found the limited space stifling. She missed the meadow behind her house leading into the woods, where she could freely ride Vala.

At least I could take Vala with me, she thought. When she'd first heard she might be called to court after her sister's death, Meira had protested, first thinking of her ebony horse and having to leave her behind. Vala had been a gift, one of the last she'd received from her mother. Knowing how much the horse meant to her, however, her father had agreed to have the horse brought with them to the house, where there was a small stable to keep her in.

A knock at the door pulled Meira out of her thoughts. Lyssa, a servant girl about Meira's age, answered the door, her voice too muffled to allow Meira to hear the full conversation. After a moment, the door closed, and the servant entered the room.

"Excuse me, my lord," Lyssa said. "This letter has just arrived from the castle."

Meira looked up as the servant handed the letter to her father, who sleepily rubbed at his eyes and closed the book laying on his lap. He opened the envelope and pulled the piece of parchment out, his blue eyes studying the letter carefully.

"What is it, Father?" Meira asked.

He stared at the parchment for another moment before folding it and placing it and the envelope on the table beside his chair.

"It seems that the queen regent has been made aware of our arrival already and expects us at court tomorrow," he answered after a moment.

Meira sighed, pulling her gaze away to look at the fireplace. When she and her father had discussed her taking Eirian's place at court, her father had said she wouldn't be required to attend every council meeting, and it might even be a few days before she would be expected to make her first appearance at court. Instead, she was already being called, with hardly any time to adjust to her new normal. She flexed her fingers, trying to ignore the resentment building up inside her. It wasn't her father's fault, and it was hardly Eirian's fault, but Meira couldn't help her frustration.

"We're expected to be there early in the morning," her father continued. "Apparently, Queen Regent Averith has some sort of announcement to make that she wants us all to be there for."

Meira nodded, stretching her arms as she stood. She walked over to her father, bending down to kiss him on the cheek. "I'm going to bed. I'll see you in the morning."

* * *

Meira and her father arrived at the castle early the next day and were led into the throne room. Noblemen and women lined up in the throne room, dressed in elegant jackets and dresses. Long white columns stood in each corner of the room. Three golden chandeliers hung from the ceiling high above. Two golden thrones sat upon the dais, and overhead, a balcony with a set of stairs led down to the throne room.

The noblewomen stood on one side of the throne room's main aisle, listening to their whispers amongst themselves. Some wondered aloud what the announcement could be, others speculated if the crown prince, Prince Gaelen, had anything to do with the announcement.

Trumpets blared, and everyone turned their attention toward the dais as Queen Regent Averith stood at the top of the staircase, decked out in a long black dress decorated with gleaming pearls, her long black hair blending in with the dress, showing she was still mourning for King Torryn. Some members of the crowd bowed their heads as she came to the bottom of the steps and made her way toward the dais. It was Meira's first time truly seeing the queen regent this close, and it brought a shiver to her spine, though she wasn't sure why.

The trumpets sounded again, and Prince Gaelen appeared on the balcony. Everyone in the crowd bowed their heads as he began his descent down the staircase. He wore a black tunic with the crest of Alythia embroidered into its left shoulder, a shield with three swords crossed together. His mahogany hair was trimmed short, and he wore a simple golden crown.

Prince Gaelen moved to the dais, standing next to it with his hands behind his back. As Meira watched their movements, her and Gaelen's eyes met. The prince's eyes widened, and a smile tugged at his lip before he blanked his face and turned his attention away from her, following his stepmother to the dais. Meira's heart pounded unexpectedly at the thought of seeing him again after so many years.

"My lords and ladies, thank you for coming," Queen Averith began. "I have asked you all here to inform you that I will be hosting a ball within a fortnight to welcome all the new courtiers to the castle and to celebrate the end of the mourning period for our dearly departed King Torryn. This ball will be an event unlike any other, and I hope you and your families will all attend."

Noblewomen standing around Meira whispered to each other. She listened as they talked about Gaelen and whether any of them would get a chance to dance with the prince at the ball, or even be chosen by the prince as a bride. Meira knew she wasn't wealthy or well-connected enough to even be considered as the prince's bride. Besides, who knew how much the prince remembered of her and the time they'd spent together?

The crowd bowed as the queen and prince left the dais

and disappeared out of the throne room, the crowd beginning to disperse after they'd gone.

Meira wandered the castle halls, eventually making her way out into the otherwise empty courtyard. Three targets had been set up in the center of the courtyard, with a bow and a quiver full of arrows sitting nearby. Her fingers itched to have a bow in her hands—did she dare pick it up?

She walked toward the quiver lying on the bench. She glanced up, searching the courtyard for any sign of guards. Seeing no one, she pulled one of the arrows from the quiver, picked up the bow, and placed the arrow into the arrow rest, her fingers wrapping eagerly around the bow's grip.

Taking a deep breath, Meira turned toward the target, sitting about fifteen yards away with a few arrows already in it. She loosed the arrow, letting it fly toward the target, and it whooshed through the air, hitting the target squarely on the line encircling the center. Meira smiled in satisfaction, taking another arrow from the quiver. She sent the arrow flying again, and this time it hit the target's center.

Behind her, clapping sounded. She whirled around to find Prince Gaelen sitting on the bench where the quiver had been. Meira gasped, dropping the bow to the ground.

"Your Highness, I apologize," she said. "I did not realize you were here."

Prince Gaelen smiled, stood, and walked toward her. "There's no need to apologize, my lady. It's refreshing to see someone besides me practicing here," he said. "Your archery has improved since we last met, Lady Meira."

Meira's breath caught in her throat as her cheeks flushed and she made eye contact with the prince. It was Prince Gaelen, after all, who'd introduced her to archery on that same visit they'd chattered most of the day about books.

"I . . . thank you, Your Highness," she replied softly. She bent down to pick the bow up. "I shouldn't have used your arrows and bow without permission."

Gaelen shook his head. "Nonsense. I have plenty of arrows," he said. "We'll have to practice together some time while you're here at court."

"I'd like that very much, Your Highness," Meira said.

"Gaelen!"

Meira and Gaelen both turned toward one of the entrances of the courtyard. Queen Averith stood there, surrounded by four guards, her arms crossed over her chest. Meira glanced at Gaelen as he let out a sigh, turning back to Meira.

"I have to go," he said, placing a hand on top of hers as he took the bow from her with a smile. "I hope to see you at the ball, Lady Meira." Gaelen picked up his quiver still laying on the bench and turned, walking over to his stepmother.

Though she couldn't quite make out what was being said, the prince's posture quickly changed. Chewing on her inner lip, she kept herself at a respectful distance from the conversation as she headed for the covered walkway leading back into the castle.

". . . attend the council meetings. . . " Gaelen said, but Meira could make out nothing else.

As Meira entered the walkway, she glimpsed Gaelen out of the corner of her eye. Though she hadn't heard the whole conversation, the prince's raised voice and gestures were enough to give off his frustration with the queen regent. With a huff of his chest, Gaelen turned away from his stepmother and walked back into the castle, going the opposite way from Meira.

CHAPTER TWO

Meira stepped out of her father's carriage, gazing up at the castle and its spired, spiraling towers as she nearly tripped over her ballgown. Despite her best efforts to keep the gown as simple as possible, it still didn't look much different from any of the other attendees' gowns, though at least hers didn't look like it could swallow her whole. Meira's gown was a floor-length gray-blue gown, with a flared tulle skirt and gauzy off-the-shoulder sleeves. She wore a single white pearl on a simple silver chain around her neck, a necklace that had belonged to her mother.

"Careful, Meira," her father's voice said, gently placing a hand on her arm and bringing her out of her thoughts. "We can't have you breaking your ankle before you've had a chance to dance with all those suitors."

Meira looked up at her father and met his gentle smile with a laugh as she placed her hand on his wrinkled one. "The only one I plan to dance with is you," she said.

Eirian would've had no problem finding someone to dance with; she was the social butterfly of the two sisters, always gossiping and flirting. Meira would rather be curled up in front of a fire at home, listening to one of her father's stories, or in the woods shooting her bow and arrow than attend this ball. The only thing that might save her from an unbearably awkward night was seeing Prince Gaelen again.

Meira had finally started to feel more at home since arriving in the capital city two weeks prior. She'd found herself some structure, waking up early each morning, commuting by carriage to the castle and arriving at court. She had spent most of her time there, being introduced to some noblewomens' daughters by her cousin, Haelyn, and learning the general daily routine she'd have as a member of court attending council meetings.

When it was just the two of them, Haelyn played nice, but as soon as some of the other nobility approached them, Meira's cousin acted as though they weren't related at all. She did her best to ignore her cousin's behavior, though she couldn't ignore the hurt she felt from it. Haelyn was, after all, the closest thing she had left to an older sister.

In Meira's spare time, she visited the bookshop she and her father had gone to on the afternoon of their arrival and explored the city. She hadn't spoken to Prince Gaelen since her first day at court, though she'd seen him from a distance, usually speaking to some of the younger noblemen around his age.

Meira climbed the steps with growing trepidation, bracing herself for an uneventful night of watching the nobility dance. Her dress pressed against her legs and she hid a frown. The sooner the night ended, the sooner she'd be freed from the itchy ball gown and back in the comfort of her own clothes.

Matching footmen opened the gilded doors to the ball-room, and a butler watched with critical eyes as she smoothed her skirt with sweaty palms. But her nerves were forgotten as the ballroom opened before her. A swirl of noblemen and women streaming past like a cloud of bright butterflies, the orchestra's music drowning out their chatter, and a sudden desire to join them filled her. Her father hooked his arm through hers as they entered. Warm air hit Meira almost immediately as she stepped in. She forced herself to stay where she was, resisting the urge to retreat to her father's carriage.

Meira surveyed the room. Golden chandeliers hung high above from a vaulted ceiling, painted with scenes of the kingdom's history—something that must have taken *years* to do, Meira thought. Straight ahead was the grand staircase leading to a balcony. Below it was a dais with two golden thrones. Orchestra musicians sat tucked into the far left corner, waiting to begin playing their first waltz of the night.

Strong of root, strong of thorn, she thought, reciting her family motto. *I can do this.*

Her father squeezed her arm, giving her a gentle smile. "I have to speak with one of the council members for a few minutes," he said, then vanished into the crowd.

Dancers gathered at the bottom of the staircase as the court herald stood nearby. Meira made her way over to one of the nearby walls by the ballroom's entrance, resting her back against it.

"Presenting her royal majesty, Queen Regent Averith, and His Royal Highness Prince Gaelen!" the herald announced.

Queen Regent Averith stood at the top of the staircase, decked out in an obsidian gown, her long dark hair blending in with the elegant dress. The queen flitted down the stairs like a shadow. Members of the crowd bowed their heads as she came to the bottom of the steps, then parted, giving the queen a path to the ballroom's center. The queen regent walked toward the dais, where two empty thrones sat. A shiver ran down Meira's spine as she watched the queen, thinking back to that moment in the courtyard with Prince Gaelen a few weeks prior and how angry the queen had seemed.

Meira turned her gaze back to the top of the staircase, where Prince Gaelen stood. Her heart fluttered as he searched the crowd, pausing halfway down the steps, and she wondered if he'd noticed her.

The prince wore a black tunic with the kingdom's crest embroidered into it and a golden crown atop his head. After surveying the room, he followed behind the queen regent to the dais and remained standing. As soon as the queen was seated, the music began playing, and dancers made their way back into the room's center.

Meira looked up as Haelyn approached her, wearing a golden ball gown decorated with flowers all along the bottom, with her blonde hair twisted into a bun with locks of curls hanging from it.

"Meira, you look lovely," her cousin greeted.

Meira smiled, pulling her gaze from the dancers. "So do you, Haelyn. Your gown is lovely," she said.

"Thank you," Haelyn replied. She turned to face the dancers in the center of the room. "You're not planning on being a wallflower all night, are you?"

Meira shifted uncomfortably at her cousin's question, pulling herself away from the wall. "Actually, I was just about to go find my father and ask him for the dance he owes me," she replied. With that, Meira walked away, moving farther onto the dance floor.

She strode over to where her father stood, talking to a

fellow councilman. Her father looked at her and gave a soft smile, offering his hand to her. "If you'll excuse me, Lord Weylin, I believe I owe my lovely daughter here a dance," he said.

Meira placed her hand into her father's, letting him lead her into the center of the dance floor. He placed his free hand on her waist, beginning to step in tune with the music as he held her close.

"What do you think of the ball so far?" he asked.

Meira smiled. "It's pretty much what I expected. Lots of women dancing in puffy dresses, flirting with lots of men," she answered. "At least I'm dressed to match."

Her father chuckled. "You are, at that. But you look lovelier than all the other women in the ballroom, my dear," he said affectionately. "I do hope you find someone else to dance with besides your father, though."

"I might be able to help with that, Lord Daesyn."

Meira stopped dancing as soon as she heard Prince Gaelen's voice behind her. She slowly turned, catching her breath as Gaelen's eyes met hers. She shyly reached up to tuck a curly strand of hair behind her ear, lowering her gaze.

"Lord Daesyn, I was wondering if I might have the honor of this dance with your lovely daughter?" Gaelen asked, bowing his head.

Meira looked up at Gaelen with a smile, then to her father. The councilor gazed at her with affection as he bent down and kissed her on the cheek. He released her hand, stepping away from her and Gaelen.

"Go ahead," he said with a smile. "My old bones could use a break from dancing."

Meira caught her breath as her father left her alone with Gaelen, her heart pounding. For a moment, she forgot about all the other people in the room, the musicians playing softly as they tuned up their instruments for the next piece, the quiet chatter of polite conversation and gossip. Gaelen had never looked quite so. . . dashing, like a hero stepped straight from a storybook. His hair was brushed back beneath the crown he wore, and his eyes flashed with a sort of wisdom—like that of a future king.

All at once, their surroundings returned to her awareness. She couldn't shake the feeling of eyes watching her, watching them, and a sense of jealous anger from some of the girls. She caught a glimpse of Haelyn, glaring at Meira out of the corner of her eye over a laced fan. Meira's lips curled into a smile in triumph as the prince came closer.

Gaelen bowed his head, gently raising the back of her hand to plant a soft kiss. Meira's heart raced, tuning out the other noises of the ballroom. Everything was happening so fast. She and Gaelen had only just reunited a few weeks prior and had barely seen each other since. Now here he was in front of her, asking her to dance. . . it felt natural, like their time apart had been nothing at all.

"May I have the honor of this dance?" he asked with a sweeping bow, keeping her hand in his.

Meira held her breath and nodded, letting the prince lead her to the center of the ballroom. Gaelen kept his eyes on her, slowly placing a hand at Meira's waist. Meira swallowed back her nerves and reached a hand out to his shoulder. Her mind went blank as she tried to remember the proper way of dancing with someone—where did his hands go? Where did hers belong? How would she keep from tripping over her feet or dress as they danced?

The orchestra began playing a slow waltz, and within seconds they were dancing. Gaelen kept in step with the music, never tearing his eyes from hers. He must have had a thousand dancing lessons as a prince, and what Meira had as a country noble paled in comparison.

Her mind flashed back to one day when they were young, and they'd been in the tower at the back of the garden. She'd been sitting on the bed, watching him swing his sword around. He turned and grinned as he teased her, sheathing his sword before reaching down to pull her up from the bed with one hand and into the tower's center, raising their hands high above their heads. The moment had only lasted for a few seconds before Gaelen let her hands go and changed the subject, stepping back to a respectful distance.

"What are you thinking about?" Gaelen asked, keeping his voice low.

Meira felt the heat rush to her cheeks as the memory faded. She shyly glanced to the side before looking back up at him. "Well. . . I was thinking about the last time we saw each other, when I was twelve. . . in the tower in the back of your garden," she answered.

Gaelen smiled, cocking his head. "I remember. I was practicing with my sword while you sat on the bed. I started teasing you and grabbed your hands and pulled you into the center of the room with me," he said.

The prince paused, pulling away from Meira while keeping one of her hands in his. He then raised their hands in the air, spinning her around before pulling her back toward him. Gaelen then took her other hand in his and raised them both above their heads, keeping them there. After a moment, they lowered their hands, and Gaelen placed his hands on her waist again.

"I'd like to think I've developed a little more charm since then," Gaelen said with a chuckle.

Meira laughed, nodding. "I think you most definitely have," she said.

The prince started dancing again, leading Meira through the remainder of the song. As they danced, Meira looked around and saw her father standing near Haelyn, watching them. Butterflies rose in her stomach.

Meira caught her breath as Gaelen spun her in a circle as the music ended and pulled her closer, their chests touching. She gazed up into his eyes, her heart pounding. Gaelen smiled down at her, reaching up to push a strand of hair behind her ear. The heat rose in her cheeks, and she knew she needed to get out into the cool air.

"Come, there's somewhere I want to bring you," Gaelen said. He led her through the crowd of dancers and toward the doors leading out into the castle garden.

The evening chill hit Meira immediately as they entered the garden, whispers trailing behind them and Haelyn still glaring daggers at her. She paused, closing her eyes and breathing it in.

"Are you all right?" Gaelen asked.

Meira opened her eyes and smiled up at him. "I'm fine, I just . . . it was rather warm in the ballroom."

Gaelen nodded, returning her smile. "I was starting to feel the same way."

"What is it you wanted to show me?" Meira asked.

Gaelen led her down the steps leading into the garden. The fragrance of honeysuckle, jasmine and lily flowers perfumed the air as they walked down several paths. They came to the end of the garden, and Gaelen paused. There, in the back of the garden, stood an unused tower—the same tower she and Gaelen would often play in as children, though the last time she'd seen it, it hadn't looked so worn down.

Gaelen led her to the entrance of the tower. They mounted the spiraling staircase in a meandering fashion, lingering on nostalgia all the while. For a moment, Meira's memories of racing him up the tower steps to hide from his tutors filled the space with life and light, despite the late hour dimness.

"I still like to come up here when I need to think," Gaelen said as they entered.

Meira stood at the top of the steps and breathed in the familiar smell of old books and dust as she looked around. The room was mostly empty, save for a bed up against the far wall, a broken chair and a desk in the corner. Gaelen walked over to the window, where a small candle sat on the windowsill, and lit it before turning to Meira.

He held out a hand and Meira went over to him, placing her hand in his and leaning against the edge of the window. He gave a soft smile, bending his head down so their foreheads touched.

"I missed you, Meira. I've thought about those times we spent together often," Gaelen said. "I'm glad you continued practicing your archery. You're a natural."

Meira lifted her head, her heart fluttering. "I missed you too, Your Highness," she said.

"Gaelen," he corrected, reaching up to stroke her cheek.

"Gaelen," she murmured.

The night air was sweet and still. She held her breath as he leaned in close, their lips inches from each other as she realized what was happening—what she *wanted* to happen. His soft lips fell to hers, and she closed her eyes, savoring the moment.

And for the first time since returning to the capital, Meira was happy to have come.

CHAPTER THREE

Meira shifted uncomfortably in the hardback wooden chair with a scowl, moving around until she finally felt somewhat comfortable. The chair sat in the back row of the audience in the council chamber. The room was circular, with a table in its center and six empty chairs set around it, one for each member of the Ivory Council and the queen regent, with a wooden barrier between the table and audience seating. Meira's father sat on her left, wearing blue robes with long sleeves as a show of his status on the council. Behind them were rows of chairs, mostly empty but slowly filling in with nobles.

"Something the matter, dear?" Lord Daesyn asked softly.

"Yes. Whoever built this chair clearly had a different idea of comfort than I," Meira replied.

Lord Daesyn chuckled, patting her arm. "Don't worry, you won't have to sit here for long. The Ivory Council will give their usual greetings to those in the audience, and Queen Regent Averith will, perhaps, say a few words before letting everyone in the audience go," he said. "The real important discussions only include members of the council."

"Shouldn't you be up there as well?" Meira asked.

"Usually, yes. Since you are in training to take my place, I thought it important for us to observe one of the council meetings together, so I asked the council to allow me to sit with you," her father replied.

Meira nodded, trying not to think of all the future council meetings she'd be sitting in on, without her father at her side.

As she waited for the meeting to start, Meira thought back to the night of the ball, which had only taken place a few nights prior to the meeting. She smiled to herself, remembering the taste of Gaelen's lips on hers as they shared their first kiss in the garden tower. After spending a while longer in the tower, Gaelen had led her back to the ballroom. As they walked to the ballroom's center, Meira had glanced over to her cousin Haelyn, who was standing with some of the other court ladies. Her cousin's mouth was gaped open in surprise, and Meira couldn't help the grin she flashed at her cousin. Meira turned her attention back to Gaelen as the crowd made room and he led her to the center of the ballroom so they could share one last dance.

The chamber doors by the dais opened, and four Ivory Council members wearing long robes of different colors entered, each standing behind their chairs at the table, leaving two chairs open. A moment later, Queen Averith entered, and the audience members rose, watching as the queen climbed the steps of the dais and sat in the empty chair in the middle, where she could look out directly at the audience.

Each of the High Council members as stood straight-backed behind their chairs. Meira counted each member of the High Council, remembering each position—Magister, Archseer, High General, Envoy, then the queen regent. But Gaelen was nowhere to be found.

"Where is Prince Gaelen? Doesn't he belong to the Ivory Council, as the crown prince?" Meira asked.

Abruptly, everyone's eyes were on Meira. Some audience members around her had audibly gasped, others whispering quietly to each other. Queen Regent Averith stared Meira down from where she sat on the dais. Meira resisted the urge to duck down into her chair, suddenly realizing that perhaps she'd asked her question a little *too* loudly.

"The crown prince cannot attend today's meeting. He has other things to attend to," Queen Averith said coolly.

Meira swallowed hard, straightening in her chair as she looked at the queen. "I do apologize, Your Majesty. I did not mean for my question to offend you."

The queen nodded, her eyes still hard as she placed her arms on the table in front of her. "Now, perhaps we can get on with the meeting."

* * *

Meira left the council chamber a short time later, pausing outside the door to suck in a deep breath. The chamber seemed unnaturally hot after Meira's brief encounter with the queen, and she couldn't wait to get out of there. Her father had been asked to stay by the queen regent, and she only hoped her speaking out of turn wouldn't lead to him facing any repercussions.

As Meira turned down the hall, two noblewomen followed and moved past her down the hallway. Turning the corner, she entered the courtyard, stepping out into the fresh air and sunlight.

The courtyard was bustling with activity, with guards and knights drilling swordplay and archery. She looked over to where she'd spoken to Prince Gaelen a few days ago and saw him right where she'd thought he'd be, bow and arrows in hand. A few knights stood by, watching their prince.

The kiss she'd shared with Gaelen lingered in the forefront of her mind. Mere memory of the moment brought a fluttering feeling to her stomach, a warm tingle emanating throughout her body as she watched him.

The prince lined up his projectile on the bow's arrow shelf, placing one foot in front of the other as he pulled back the drawstring. A single breath. It then released with a *twang*. The arrow sailed through the air and directly into the middle of the target. A few of the knights cheered, clapping Gaelen on the shoulder.

Meira smiled, making her way toward the bench where his quiver leaned. She sat down, watching Gaelen as he talked with the other knights with a broad grin. One of the knights said something Meira couldn't quite hear, and Gaelen threw his head back, his laughter filling the courtyard. Haelyn and a few of the other noble daughters wandered beneath the covered walkway, pointing in Gaelen's direction.

Gaelen turned away from the other knights and toward the bench, making eye contact with Meira. Meira smiled, her heart fluttering.

"Meira," Gaelen greeted. He sat next to her, leaning over to give her a kiss on the cheek. "I was hoping you'd find your way out here again."

Her cheeks flushed hot as he kissed her cheek, turning

on the bench to face him. "Hello, Gaelen. And why would you be hoping for that?"

"Well, I was hoping you'd join me in archery practice, but now I think I have other plans," Gaelen answered with a chuckle. He leaned in with another kiss, this time full on the lips.

Meira inhaled as they kissed, enjoying the taste of his lips. She closed her eyes, leaning her forehead against his, suddenly forgetting that knights and guards surrounded them in the courtyard.

Gaelen pulled away after a moment, turning his head and seeing the onlooking knights standing nearby. He cleared his throat, straightening his posture as he took Meira's hand into his and pulled her from the bench.

"Perhaps we can go somewhere more private to practice," he suggested. "There's a spot in the forest I enjoy going to."

A shy laugh escaped Meira as he tugged her to her feet. "I'd like that very much."

* * *

After retrieving Vala a while later, Meira rode along the private trail through the forest behind , her long, braided hair bouncing against her back as she rode. She breathed in the fresh air and scent of new growth, grateful to be away from the confining halls of the castle and stifling expectations of court. Spending time with Gaelen was the superior option any day, especially if she could do so without the eyes of court women staring at them. Riding through the forest gave them privacy, save for the small escort of guards who trailed behind them at a safe distance.

Gaelen sat back in his saddle, his horse easing from a

comfortable lope and into a walk so she could catch up. They rode beneath a juniper tree, its long branches coming down just above their heads. Gaelen gave his horse's reins a light tug, reaching up and pulling a sprig of juniper with clusters of fragrant blue berries, handing it to Meira.

Meira smiled bashfully, taking the twig and placing it in the pouch on her waist.

"How are you enjoying life at court?" Gaelen asked.

Meira resisted the urge to roll her eyes, looking straight ahead on the path. "It's more or less what I expected," she said.

"Mindless gossip and boring meetings?" Gaelen asked with a chuckle.

Meira laughed uncomfortably. "Pretty much," she said.

Gaelen glanced back at her over a shoulder. "Is something wrong? Someone at court troubling you?"

"No, no one in particular. It's just. . . well, there are rumors."

"Ha! There are always rumors. Don't pay them any mind."

Meira twisted the reins between her fingers before finding the right words to press back Gaelen's advice. "I'm afraid I don't have quite the same luxury to ignore such things as you, Your Highness."

Gaelen slowed until she was riding slowly behind him on the trail. "What do you mean?"

"It's just that. . . well, the rumors are ones of impropriety." She flushed a little as she glanced at Gaelen's puzzled expression. "Impropriety between us. . ." she added.

"And?" He still didn't see any problem.

Meira grimaced a little and looked away. He was really going to make her spell it out for him. "If my integrity as a woman is under suspicion, it will be difficult for me to find a husband in the coming years. My father has no other children."

"I don't think it will be difficult." There was a teasing smile on his face. "I think you have already found a young man willing to be your husband." He winked at her, then urged his horse to a swifter pace, forcing her to follow or be left behind.

Meira stared at Gaelen's back for a moment before spurring Vala into a run to catch up with the prince.

After a few minutes of riding, Meira caught up to Gaelen, entering an open clearing. She barely noticed the waterfall thundering into an otherwise peaceful lake straight ahead.

"Gaelen, do you really mean to marry me. . . ?" Breathless and flushed from the vigorous ride, Meira dismounted and walked around Vala to stare at her prince, daring to hope that he would say yes while trying to not let the queen's disapproval fuel her doubt.

"Of course I do."

"But. . . you haven't made any announcement of your intentions, and. . . and your stepmother. . ."

"What about my stepmother?" Gaelen's smile was suddenly replaced by a scowl.

"I think I upset the queen this morning when I asked why you weren't at the council meeting. She said you had other things to attend to, so I was rather surprised to see you practicing in the courtyard after."

Gaelen's posture tensed, his eyes flickering. "She has a habit of twisting the truth for her own benefit." He paused, taking her hands into his. "Meira, I intend to marry you. I thought that was obvious. Averith won't allow me to announce my wish to court you, but that does not stop me from courting you." He pouted his lips. "Do you not want me to court you, Meira?"

Meira's eyes widened. "Of course I do, Gaelen. It's just. . . being so new to court, I feel a bit like an outsider, trying to find where I fit in." She sighed, turning her gaze away. "My sister was far more suited for life at court than I."

Gaelen smiled, giving her hands a gentle squeeze. "I don't think you give yourself enough credit. From what I've seen, court life suits you rather well." His smile faded. "How has your father been since his sickness and Eirian's death? Our paths don't cross very often when he's at court, so I've not had the chance to speak to him."

"He's doing better than he was when he first took ill, but it weakened him," Meira answered. "He still misses my mother dearly. . . and Eirian."

"I remember your sister. I was sorry to hear about her. She and your cousin, I believe, were always trying to catch my attention," Gaelen said after a moment. He squeezed her hands, studying Meira's expression. He grinned at her in an obvious attempt to lighten the mood. "But I was still thinking about a certain redhead instead."

Meira blushed, lifting her gaze to make eye contact with him.

His grin broadened as he raised the back of her hand to his lips, planting a soft kiss. "Come on, there's something I want to show you."

Gaelen led her toward the lake, stopping by the water's edge. Meira looked around, watching as the water fell over large rocks in mesmerizing ripples. She leaned against Gaelen's side, comfortable in his presence and their solitude.

"It's so. . . peaceful here," Meira said.

"I like coming here when I want to be alone, and to get

away from my stepmother and her multitude of rules," Gaelen explained. "Of course, one of her rules is to *not* leave the castle grounds, but my knights and guards are loyal to me. They know I come here and won't betray my trust."

"You don't get along with her, do you?" Meira asked.

Gaelen shook his head. "No. Ever since my father died, she's been. . . different. Colder, more restrictive. At least, more restrictive of what she thinks my routine should be." He leaned toward Meira and kissed her on the cheek. "But she can't keep me from doing what I want forever. Or from spending as much time as I can with you, for that matter."

Heat rose to Meira's cheeks as she turned to fully face him. "You know, I didn't want to come back to court. I felt almost. . . resentful of my sister for leaving the responsibility of taking my father's place to me when I wanted no part of it, even knowing it wasn't her fault." She paused, giving him a shy smile. "But now, I'm glad I came. I don't know what I expected when I came to court, but I never thought I'd reconnect with you, or that it would lead to me standing here with you, out in the wilderness."

Gaelen pulled her closer, wrapping an arm around her waist while stroking her cheek with his other hand. "I'm glad you did too," he said, leaning in to kiss her again.

Meira closed her eyes as they kissed, savoring the taste of his lips again. *I could get used to this*, she thought.

"I want to shout to the world that you and I are together," Gaelen murmured against her lips.

Meira smiled into the kiss. "As do I."

* * *

After their ride through the forest, Meira and Gaelen strolled through the garden, discussing their recent outings. They rounded a corner and headed down one of the many rows of flowers, hand in hand. Up ahead, Meira saw her father and the queen walking down the same pathway. Meira glanced at Gaelen, wondering if they should drop their hands, but even as they approached, Gaelen didn't loosen his grip. Instead, his fingers tightened on hers. Just a bit, but enough.

"Stepmother, Lord Daesyn," Gaelen greeted. He stopped near one of the garden's many water fountains, a circular marble pool with three spouts pouring water softly into it.

"My prince," Meira's father greeted, bowing his head. "It's a lovely day for a stroll through the garden." He looked at Meira. "Your Majesty, may I introduce my daughter, Meira? Although it appears that Meira and the crown prince have already become well acquainted," he added with a smile. "She has come to take her older sister's place at court."

Gaelen's fingers tightened a bit more on Meira's. Meira glanced up at the prince, noticing that his posture had changed as she was introduced to the queen—his back straightened, his eyes watching the queen carefully. Meira gave his hand a reassuring squeeze before looking back at the queen.

"Your Majesty," she said. She curtsied and bowed her head.

"You may, indeed, Lord Daesyn," the queen regent said. Meira looked up at the queen, whose eyes stared back at her with a silent judgment in them. "You were at this morning's council meeting. Tell me, did you attend the ball the other night, Lady Meira? Did you enjoy it?"

Meira raised her chin, noticing the tone in the queen's voice. She dared not look at Gaelen to see his reaction, not wanting to provoke him into causing a scene.

"I was. And yes, I did, thank you, Your Majesty," Meira answered carefully. "It was a beautiful night."

"It was indeed," Queen Averith said. "If you'll excuse us, Lord Daesyn and I are due to attend another council meeting shortly."

Meira and Gaelen shifted to the side as Queen Averith strode past them. Meira's father leaned over to kiss Meira on the cheek, glancing at Prince Gaelen. "Enjoy your stroll, Meira."

Meira watched out of the corner of her eye as the queen walked past her, holding her breath. The reflection in the fountain's water stirred, and Meira glanced over, watching. The queen's pretty complexion had been replaced by that of a woman with pointed ears sticking out beneath long black hair, her eyes dark, surrounded by shadows moving all around her. Meira blinked, trying to shake the image from her vision. By the time she looked back at the water, the queen's reflection had changed back.

"Something wrong?" Gaelen asked, tugging her back onto the main path of the garden.

"No, it's nothing. I thought I saw something in the water, but I think it was just a trick of the light," she answered as they continued along the path.

Gaelen paused by one of the rose bushes nearby, releasing Meira's hand. He pulled at the stem of a blush-pink rose, yanking it from the bush and handing it to Meira, careful of its thorns. She smiled as she took the rose, holding it close to inhale its fragrance before placing it at her belt.

"I saw my cousin Haelyn and some of the other noble daughters in the courtyard this morning, practically fawning over you. I suspect that, if she'd had the chance,

Haelyn would have asked you to dance at the ball," Meira said.

"Do I detect a hint of jealousy, Lady Meira?" Gaelen asked with a chuckle.

"Me, jealous?" Meira asked, feigning shock. "Never."

"Well, as far as I'm concerned, all those other noblemen can have her. There's only one girl for me," Gaelen said.

"Oh, and who's that?" Meira asked with a teasing smile.

"Oh, just some princess from another kingdom. She and I danced at the ball. In fact, my stepmother is already in talks with her father about marriage," he replied, his tongue teasingly darting out between his teeth.

Meira's eyes widened, and she reached both her hands out to grab his. "They better not be. Otherwise, I may just have to go find a different suitor," she said with a laugh. Meira knew he was teasing, but she couldn't help a jolt of jealousy at the thought of him even pretending interest in another girl. In the back of her mind, though, Meira knew the truth—political marriages among royalty between different kingdoms could become an obstacle for her relationship with Gaelen. If a princess from another kingdom came along and bid for marriage to Gaelen, Meira knew she had no true standing.

"And just what are you going to do about it, Lady Meira?" he asked.

Meira tilted her head. He laughed, leaning his head forward so their heads touched. "You're cute when you're jealous, you know," he said. "Even if you have nothing to be jealous of."

Meira felt his hot breath again as he breathed and their lips inches from each other. He pressed them against Meira's, and she closed her eyes. After a moment, their lips parted, and she pulled back to look up at him.

"Haelyn could hardly believe it when she saw me dancing with you at the ball, you know," Meira said.

"Well, I guess we certainly showed her, didn't we?" Gaelen said with a laugh. "You and your father seem close. It's nice to see."

Meira smiled. "My father was who I got my love of books from, actually. I love sitting in front of the fireplace, listening to his stories. He taught me horseback riding and gave me lessons after you showed me archery when we were twelve. What about you?" Meira asked.

His face changed to a pained expression. Meira chewed hard on the inside of her lip, realizing that she had, perhaps, brought up a touchy subject.

"Well, as you know, my father passed away nearly two years ago," Gaelen answered. "When my stepmother first came to the castle, she'd make a comment or two toward me. But since my father's passing, she's become... difficult to deal with. Her cruelty toward me has become more personal and made it harder to ignore."

Gaelen turned his head to look out into the distance, his eyes sad. Meira considered asking him more about it but then thought better of it, remembering the feeling of underlying tension between the two of them a few days prior. Perhaps it was better not to press him further.

They rounded another corner, coming close to a water fountain in the center of the garden. A glimmering light in one of the nearby bushes caught Meira's eye, and she frowned. She blinked, shaking her head slightly. Meira glanced up at Gaelen, who didn't seem to notice. As they walked a bit farther, she heard a soft laugh, almost like tiny bells. Where was it coming from?

They reached the water fountain in the center. Gaelen and Meira sat on its edge, Meira dipping her fingers into the water. She heard little bells again and looked around, eyes wide.

"What is it?" Gaelen asked, confused.

Tiny lights danced in a nearby bush, and now Meira *knew* she had seen something. She watched them cautiously until, finally, they disappeared.

"Did you see those little dancing lights over by the flowers?" Meira asked.

"Little dancing lights?" Gaelen asked. "Oh, you mean the fireflies? I've seen them lots of times around here in the garden. The oasis is said to be full of them at nighttime. They're quite beautiful."

Meira thought back to what her father had told her about the oasis on the way to the city. She smiled, turning to look up at him. "It sounds beautiful. Maybe we can go see them together some time," she said.

"I would like that," Gaelen said. "I had a really nice time today, Meira."

She smiled as Galen tilted her chin up, leaning up to meet him. "Me too."

* * *

That night, Meira rode in Gaelen's carriage through the city, once more heading toward the oasis. Gaelen had come to her door earlier that evening, offering her a stunning scarlet rose and a romantic carriage ride through the city. After her father had given his encouragement for her to go, Meira had happily accepted the rose, taking his offered hand and stepping into the carriage. She'd asked where they were going, but Gaelen refused to tell her, saying it was a surprise.

After leaving Gaelen at the castle that afternoon, Meira

had returned to the house in the city and entered her father's small library, looking for a book that might contain information on the dancing lights she'd seen. Though Gaelen had called them fireflies, Meira suspected there was more to them than that—after all, it was far too early in the afternoon for fireflies to be anywhere in sight, and they were the wrong color.

She gazed out the window as they moved farther from the city and toward the oasis along the same road that, if she wanted to, would lead her home, to the house she'd been born and grown up with Eirian in.

The sky had begun turning a brilliant orange, preparing for a vibrant sunset as the carriage came to a halt by the side of the road. The coachman opened the door, offering a hand to help Meira out of the carriage. Once she'd stepped out, Gaelen followed, offering a hand for her to take.

"Gaelen, where are you taking me?" Meira asked with a laugh.

"You'll see," he replied with a very intentionally mysterious air, teasing. He led her toward a moss-covered stone wall and to the other side of it to the well. Vines and tiny glowing flowers surrounded the outside of the well, blending in with overgrown grass. As they approached it, Meira knew immediately where she was. The well looked abandoned, but at the same time, Meira could tell it was well tended to in a naturalistic fashion.

Meira leaned over the edge, staring down into the endless black hole before she looked around. "It's beautiful."

"I thought it would make a great spot for a view of the sunset and fireflies," Gaelen said. He raised her hand to his lips to touch the back of it. "Plus, I wanted to see you again."

Meira laughed. "You just saw me this afternoon. You missed me that much?" she asked, smiling.

Gaelen nodded, leading her away from the well and toward the grassy area of the oasis. The coachman brought a folded blanket to Gaelen, who took it and laid it out on the grass. Meira settled on the blanket and Gaelen followed, sitting behind her so she could rest against him.

The bright orange sun dimmed, slipping out of existence as the brilliant blue night sky took its place, filling with stars. As the night sky made its appearance, Meira looked out into the grasslands, waiting for the fireflies to make their appearance.

"You said you had seen the fireflies before, in your garden?" Meira asked.

"Yes. The first time I noticed them, it wasn't long after my father married Averith. But I've seen them a few other times since then, even during the day," Gaelen answered.

Meira watched the fireflies continue to slowly appear, rising out of the grass and bouncing around in the sky. She cocked her head to one side as she watched them. The fireflies weren't just their usual yellow color—some were purple, some were pink, some green. How odd. She thought back to when she was a child, chasing fireflies through the grass by her house with her sister. Those fireflies had been their flickering yellow. There was something different about these fireflies—magical.

"Gaelen. . . what if those aren't fireflies?" Meira asked suddenly. She sat up and turned on the blanket to face him.

"What do you mean? What else could they be?" Gaelen asked.

Meira stood up, pulling Gaelen up by the hand, and led him back over to the well. "What if they're *not* fireflies?" she repeated, peering into the well. "What if they're fairies?"

Gaelen raised a skeptical eyebrow. "Fairies?"

"Yes, fairies. I've read books about them. . . I didn't think they were more than stories, but they say that fairies can change what they look like to humans," Meira explained. "They say that the well was blessed by a fairy, yes? What if Averith made a deal with a fairy?"

Gaelen stared at Meira, but a look of realization dawned. "I. . . suppose it's possible," he said skeptically. "I do admit that I've felt as though something is. . . off about Averith. Even my father felt that way after they were first married. He said it was like an invisible veil had been placed over the kingdom by her."

Meira nodded. "I'll have to do some more reading, but. . . maybe there's some kind of lore that could help."

Gaelen inhaled and nodded. Keeping her hand in his, she pressed her lips against his in a kiss.

* * *

That night, Meira sat at the desk in her room, humming softly to herself as she placed the juniper sprig Gaelen had given her on the desk in front of her. She then picked a pin up, keeping it straight in her hand as she placed the juniper against it. She laid them together on the desk, tucking a long piece of yarn beneath them. After cutting the yarn, she carefully tied it around the juniper and sprig, tightening them together and making sure it was secure. Smiling, she sniffed the juniper, inhaling its scent, and let the fragrance implant in her memory as one she would forever associate with Gaelen.

CHAPTER FOUR

Meira sat in on another dreadfully dull meeting, anxiously waiting for it to end so she could slip away and find Gaelen. The queen regent and council members had been going back and forth about some dispute involving trade routes over the northern mountains for a while now, and Meira could hardly take it anymore. She twisted her sweaty fingers in her lap, desperately hoping it would end soon.

When the Magister finally adjourned the meeting, Meira sprang up from the uncomfortable chair and walked out of the council chamber, thankful to finally relax.

"Lady Meira, a moment of your time."

Meira paused by the door and turned as Queen Averith approached, instead placing her hands behind her back. Queen Averith's long, curly hair had been twisted into elegant braids pinned against her head, loose strands left to artfully hang. She wore a strange black lipstick and a forest green dress.

Meira's clothing was far less elegant—a light-blue tunic with short, loose sleeves, with the juniper sprig pin she'd made pinned to the left part of her tunic. She bowed her head, giving the queen a soft smile. "Your Majesty," she greeted. "What may I do for you?"

"Would you walk with me for a moment, my dear?" the queen asked.

Meira inclined her head deferentially. "Of course."

The queen looped her arm around Meira's and walked down the hallway, pulling Meira distressfully close to her as they went. Meira hid her surprise at the gesture and sucked in a thin breath, keeping her gaze straight as they walked, and she hid the brief flash of fear.

"I noticed the pin on your tunic. Where did you get it? It's lovely," Queen Averith asked.

"Thank you. Prince Gaelen gave me the sprig, and I made it into a pin," Meira answered.

The queen smiled, likewise not making eye contact with her. "He seems quite smitten with you," she said.

"As I am of the prince, Your Majesty. I enjoy spending time with him," Meira replied.

"I'm not surprised. He seems to enjoy finding ways to charm the young ladies of the court," Queen Averith said.

Meira resisted the urge to stop short at the queen's words. She kept her attention on their path rather than the queen directly, mastering the twitch of expression that struggled to show openly on her face, though her fingers instinctively curled into fists in spite of herself.

"You don't seem too surprised either," the queen continued. "You've seen the way the other young ladies of the court conduct themselves around you, yes?"

Meira thought back to the two girls who had followed her as she left the council chambers on the day of her first meeting. Even Haelyn had been behaving differently toward her. She bit the inside of her lip, trying not to show the queen any confirmation of her accusations.

"I'm not quite certain what you mean, Your Majesty," Meira said.

"You're new and interesting to Gaelen and have taken the attention away from them," Queen Averith replied. "He's told each of them different lies, but the attention he's paying you now shows those lies for what they are. They're jealous and hurt by Gaelen and taking it out on you because they can't take it out on him."

For a moment, Meira wondered whether the queen was right. The other women in court ignored her. She'd seen the way Gaelen acted toward the other court women, and in the back of her mind she couldn't help but wonder. After all, he would have spent far more time with them, and even with her cousin, before she ever arrived at court. How many of them had he flirted with before she'd come along?

No. Gaelen isn't like that, she told herself firmly. *She's wrong.*

Raising her chin, Meira turned toward the queen. "I appreciate your concern, Your Majesty, but please don't feel the need to trouble yourself on my behalf," she said.

The queen gave her an unexpectedly kind, sharp smile. "Of course. Still, I encourage you to think about what I've said and whether you wish to make things worse between you and the other court women," she said. "If you'll excuse me, I have some things I need to do. It was good speaking with you, Lady Meira."

The queen strode off down the hallway, leaving Meira alone to think about what she'd said. She flexed her fingers and inhaled, aggressively pushing the negative thoughts out of her mind, wishing she hadn't even entertained what the queen had said. After a moment, she began walking down the hallway again, heading toward the castle gardens.

"Meira!"

Meira turned as her cousin approached, placing her hands behind her back as she waited for her cousin to come closer. She suppressed a sigh, wishing she'd stop being interrupted—she wanted to find and speak to Gaelen.

"Hello, Haelyn," Meira said as politely as she could manage.

"What were you and the queen talking about? Did she say anything to you about the ball?" Haelyn asked.

Meira looked back in the direction the queen had walked in, watching as the woman turned the corner before looking back at her cousin.

"Oh. . . it was nothing. She just wanted to see how I was doing since coming to court," Meira said, shaking her head.

"I see," Haelyn replied, clearly disappointed.

Meira resisted the urge to roll her eyes, knowing exactly what the elder girl's intentions were. Haelyn didn't *care* about Meira, she only wanted to gossip.

"Are you heading to the gardens?" Haelyn asked.

Meira nodded. "Yes, I'm meeting Prince Gaelen there," she said.

"Good, I'll join you. I'm meeting some of the other ladies," Haelyn said.

Meira led the way down the hall and around the corner toward the entrance to the garden. Some of the other noblewomen were waiting under the covered walkway for Haelyn and waved her over. Excusing herself, Meira entered the garden and made her way toward the tower in the back corner.

"Excuse me, Lady Meira?" a voice behind her called.

Meira turned as Declan, the captain of the prince's

guard, approached. His brow was covered in sweat, with long locks of blonde hair falling into his eyes, and he must have stood a foot over her. Meira felt small in comparison—even Gaelen didn't tower over her *that* much.

"Prince Gaelen sent me to find and inform you that he is not in the tower. He is in the family crypt and hopes you will meet him there," Declan said.

Meira raised her eyebrows in surprise. She knew Gaelen sometimes visited his father in the crypt, but why would he want her there?

"Thank you, Sir Declan. I'll go there straight away," she said after a moment.

"Of course, my lady. If you wish, I can escort you to the crypt's entrance," the knight replied, bowing his head.

Meira nodded and followed Declan back through the garden. As she trailed behind, she thought about the conversation she'd had with the queen. Should she tell Gaelen or keep it to herself? She didn't want to upset him, much less have him go rushing off to his stepmother and make the situation even more awkward. But she also didn't want to keep anything from him, either.

Declan led Meira through the stone archway leading from the garden into the courtyard and toward one of the castle walls, to a set of stone steps leading down into a dark tunnel.

"Follow the tunnel and you will find His Highness inside," Declan said.

Meira nodded, smiling at the knight. "Thank you, Declan."

Beginning her descent down the stone steps, Meira used her hand to guide her as she moved it along the cool stone wall. She entered the tunnel, finding herself in complete darkness.

"Gaelen?" Meira called out, her voice echoing in the tunnel.

"Meira, down here," Gaelen's voice called back.

Still using the wall to guide her, Meira stepped farther into the tunnel. After walking several steps, she turned a corner. Torchlight flickered along the wall up ahead, lighting her path. Following the light, she turned another corner, entering a room.

Gaelen knelt with one leg raised up, his head lowered, and resting on his knee in front of two stone statues. Looking around the room, Meira saw several stone statues spread throughout. A memory flashed in her mind as she looked at each of the statues, remembering when Gaelen brought her down there as children.

Gaelen lifted his head, looking up at Meira with a smile. "Hi," he greeted. He stood up, giving her a quick kiss.

"Hi," Meira replied, smiling back as she returned his kiss. "Were you waiting long?"

Gaelen shook his head. "No. . . I came down here a while ago, just to think and pay them a visit," he replied, nodding to the statues of his parents. "I didn't mean for you to have to meet me down here, but I lost track of time."

Meira shook her head. "That's alright. I remember you taking me down here when we were children," she said.

Gaelen took Meira's hand and led her to a stone bench sitting up against one of the walls. Meira followed, sitting down and looking around the room. She twiddled her fingers, debating whether now was a good time to bring up her encounter with the queen.

"Is something the matter?" Gaelen asked. "You seem a bit. . . distant."

Meira looked up at Gaelen, studying his features for a

moment. *Do I tell him? I don't want to upset him. . . but he should know*, she thought.

"Meira, what is it? You can tell me," Gaelen said, furrowing his eyebrows in concern.

"I just don't want it to upset you," Meira said after a moment, lowering her gaze.

"Why would whatever you have to tell me make me upset?" he asked with a concerned tone.

"Because it has to do with your stepmother," Meira answered.

Gaelen shifted his position on the bench, reaching his other hand up to run it along Meira's cheek, pushing a loose strand of hair behind her ear. "What did she say? She didn't say anything to upset you, did she?"

Meira shook her head. "No, not especially. . ."

Gaelen frowned. "Then, what is it?"

Meira sighed, looking up at him. "She suggested that the other young ladies of the court are jealous of the time that you and I spend together, and that the only reason you're interested in me is because I'm new to court," she said. "I don't believe anything she said to me, though. I know you. . . I know you aren't what she was insinuating."

Gaelen lowered his hand from her cheek, fingers curling into a fist. He stood from the bench, letting go of her hand and moving toward the tunnel entrance.

"She has no right speaking to you like that," he grumbled. "I'm going to go talk to her right now."

"Gaelen, wait," Meira said. She ran after him, grabbing his hand to pull him back toward the bench. "Don't give in to her and make a scene. I'm fine, and I know nothing she said was true. It's not worth angering her over."

Gaelen sighed, reaching up to rub his chin in frustration. Meira stepped closer to him, placing a hand on his arm.

"Promise me you won't say anything to her. I know the truth, and that's all that matters," she said.

Gaelen nodded, pulling her closer. "Alright, I won't say anything. But I don't understand why she would say anything to you *at all*, unless. . ."

"Unless what?" Meira asked.

"Unless she was trying to sabotage me," Gaelen said slowly, considering. "It would certainly fit everything she's done—making me look foolish at council meetings, telling me I'm not good enough to be king. . . even some of the noblewomen our age have acted strangely toward me at times. And she still will not allow me to formally announce my courtship to you."

Meira stared at Gaelen, unsure what to say.

He led her back to the bench, pulling her with him to sit down. "Meira, the reason I've been so invested in you is because, from the day we met as children, you saw me and liked me for *myself*, and not as a path to the crown and power. We shared something I hadn't shared with anyone before, and it made me feel less lonely," he said.

Meira smiled, keeping her hands in his as they sat down. "I felt the same way. It was nice having a friend I could talk to about books and things I enjoyed reading without being laughed at or judged," she said.

Silence fell between them for a moment. Gaelen leaned in and gave Meira a quick kiss, reaching up to push a strand of loose hair out of her face as the kiss broke.

"There's something you should know, Meira," he said after a moment. "Every ruler has the ability to magically share the ruling of the country with one other person. Most choose their spouse, but they don't have to. For Averith to have full control of the kingdom, she could share that power with me and be queen. If I were to marry before I turn twenty-one, I could take the throne immediately. I'm already twenty. But until that happens, I have to wait until I'm of age. Averith is aware of that law, and I'm sure she will do anything she can to maintain power for as long as possible."

Meira stared at Gaelen, unsure of what to say to this information. What did that mean? Was that an indirect proposal? Was he just using her to get to the crown? Her heart pounded in her chest at the thought of them getting married. She cared for Gaelen and wanted to spend as much time with him as she could. What chance did she have at marrying him, especially if Queen Averith had something to say about it? Could she truly handle the responsibility of being queen if she did?

"I don't want to scare you or make you think that I necessarily *expect* us to get married, at least not right away," Gaelen continued after a moment. "I just wanted to make you aware of the law. Knowing Averith, she will do whatever she can to keep me from marrying sooner than I have to."

Meira nodded, shyly looking up at him. "I'm. . . not totally against it, you know."

"Neither am I." He pulled her up from the bench, raising the back of her hand to his lips. "If you'd like, we can head back up to the courtyard and get some archery practice in."

Meira smiled. "I'd love that."

Keeping her hand in his, Gaelen led Meira back down the hallway and toward the crypt's entrance.

CHAPTER FIVE

Meira walked with Gaelen through the streets of the capital city, heading toward the estate house so she could retrieve Vala from the stables and she and Gaelen could go riding together. As they neared the estate, Meira pointed out the bookshop she'd visited on the first night of her arrival in the city and had picked up a book on fairy lore.

A few minutes later, they arrived, and Meira opened the door and entered the foyer of the estate, but not before allowing Gaelen to enter first. The two were immediately greeted by Lyssa, who, upon seeing the prince, bowed, muttering, "Your Highness."

"Rise, Lyssa. There is no need for all that," Meira said. "Prince Gaelen is here at my request and is my visitor."

"My lady," Lyssa responded, rising, though her head remained bowed. "Can I fetch anything for you and your guest?"

Meira shook her head, and Lyssa scurried away. She turned to Gaelen. "Would you like to see my father's library?" Meira asked. "He has quite a few Alythian history books you might be interested in."

"I'd love to," Gaelen answered.

As the Keeper of Histories, the shelves of her father's library were lined with rows of books containing everything one needed to know about the kingdom of Alythia, dating as far back as a thousand years. Most books contained logs of things like royal family members. But others—the ones Meira was more interested in—contained myths and legends of Alythia's land, including stories of the fairy folk. She'd eagerly devoured the pages of many of these books, and her father often teased that she would soon know more about Alythia's history than he did.

Gaelen looked around the room and smiled before turning back to Meira. "You weren't kidding about your father's collection being impressive," he said.

"These are just the books that aren't in his study," Meira replied with a laugh.

Gaelen walked to one of the shelves, tilting his head as he looked at the titles of each book. Meira joined him and stood by his side, looking at the title of the book he seemed focused on—*A Hundred Years of Alythian Royalty*.

Gaelen reached a hand up and pulled the book from the shelf, using one hand to hold it and another to turn the pages. After a few moments of flipping through, he stopped. His fingers traced over a portrait of a woman with long brown hair twisted into braids, wearing a silver crown with a single green jewel in its center. A silver necklace hung from her neck, with the Alythian crest hanging from it. She wore an emerald-green gown with long, flowy sleeves. Written beneath the portrait was *Queen Maristella, wife of King Torryn*. The passage about Queen Maristella's life was short, only a few paragraphs long.

"Queen Maristella. . . your mother?" Meira asked.

Gaelen nodded, his gaze sad. "I was five when she died. I barely remember her. . . mostly I remember her reading and singing to me." His voice faltered as he spoke.

Meira peered past his shoulder, looking down at the portrait. "I lost my mother shortly after I reached my tenth year. She used to read me stories about the fairy folk. I suppose that's why I've always been interested in them."

Gaelen turned the page, this time to a portrait of King Torryn. His passage was much longer. "My father wouldn't like what's happened since his passing. He wouldn't agree with anything Averith has done. . . or how she's treated me. Everything seemed to change after he passed."

Meira frowned, turning to face him. "Does she treat you that badly?"

"Not physically, but more verbally, with the things she says and tells the council members," Gaelen answered. He cleared his throat then closed the book hard and placed it back on the shelf before turning away from Meira and walking over to a wall where an oil painting of Eirian hung.

Meira watched Gaelen for a moment before following him, staring up at the painting of her sister. "I feel like everything changed after Eirian died, too," she said after a moment. "It took my father and I a while to fall into a new routine. It had been just the three of us for so long. . . and then my father got sick, and then Eirian. And then I almost lost them both."

Gaelen nodded, wrapping his arms around her in a hug. Meira returned the hug, lying her head on his chest. It was nice to have someone else to speak to about how her sister's death and father's sickness had affected her and know that they truly understood how she felt.

After a moment, Meira looked up at Gaelen with a soft smile. "How about we go get Vala and take that ride?"

Gaelen returned her smile, planting a kiss on her lips. "Sure, let's go."

* * *

It was still early in the morning when Meira returned home from taking Vala out on a ride around the bustling city. After leaving Vala with the stable hand, she went inside to find her father. She'd gone on the ride to give herself more time to think about what to say to him regarding Gaelen's intentions to marry her.

Meira found her father sitting in his chair by the fireplace. She hung her cloak and quietly shut the door behind her, making her way over to where he sat. A book lay sprawled open on his chest, his hands resting on top of it. His spectacles had slid down his nose, and his head rested back, eyes closed. Smoke rose from the logs in the fireplace, indicating that the flames had burned out quite some time ago, and her father had likely fallen asleep in his chair—a habit of his he'd never managed to break.

Meira twiddled her fingers, debating whether she should wake him. She knew she needed to at least make him aware of her conversation with Queen Averith, and with Gaelen.

Meira knelt next to her father, gently placing a hand on his arm and shaking it. He emitted a snore but quickly opened his eyes.

"Meira, what is it?" Lord Daesyn asked, trying to stifle a yawn as he sat up.

"I'm sorry, Father, I didn't want to wake you," Meira

said. "I have something important I need to talk to you about. It's about Prince Gaelen and the queen regent."

Lord Daesyn frowned, placing the book on his chest onto the table next to his chair. "What about them, bright heart?"

How was she going to approach what she needed to tell him? He might dismiss the queen's words as friendly conversation and nothing to worry about. But then, there was what she and Gaelen had seen at the oasis, and her conversation with Gaelen about the marriage law…

"Queen Averith spoke with me a few days ago after a council meeting," Meira began, pulling up a chair next to his.

Lord Daesyn nodded. "Haelyn mentioned that to me. What did she say?"

Her gaze fell to her hands. "She talked with me about Gaelen, about how the only reason he's interested in me is because I'm new to court, and that the other noble girls are jealous."

"You don't believe any of that, do you, Meira?" he asked. "I've seen the way Prince Gaelen looks at you. He seems quite captivated."

Meira smiled, looking up at him. "No, not for one minute," she said. "Gaelen cares for me, and I care for him, more than I'd ever imagined possible."

"So what are you worried about?" he asked with a laugh. "The other noble girls are just what the queen said—jealous. They'll get over it. You are the one Gaelen wants to be with."

Meira looked up at her father with a shy smile. "It's not *just* the noble girls, Father," she said. "It's something that Gaelen said."

"Oh?"

"He told me that there is a marriage law, that if he is married before he turns twenty-one, he will become king, and Queen Averith will no longer have power," she said.

Lord Daesyn raised an eyebrow. "I see. And what are your thoughts on that? Have you thought about the possibility of marrying him?"

Meira hesitated. She would be lying if she said she *hadn't* imagined herself someday walking down the aisle to Gaelen at the end of it. But that had been before the queen had said anything to her, and before Gaelen had informed her of the law.

"I have thought about it, and I want to marry him more than anything," Meira said after a moment. "But I'd be lying if I wasn't also afraid that Gaelen and the kingdom might benefit more from a marriage to someone of higher birth. He'll be expected to marry a nobleman's daughter who's used to court life, not a court outsider like me."

Lord Daesyn reached for Meira's hands, taking both of them into his rough, wrinkled ones. Giving her an affectionate smile, he shook his head. "Meira, you are so much *more* than an outsider," he said. "You are smart and brave, and you have a good head on your shoulders. The kingdom would be lucky to have you as their queen."

Her father reached a hand out to push strands of loose hair from her braid behind her ear, then raised her other hand to his lips, kissing the back of it before continuing. "Besides, who's to say a native noble wouldn't make a better queen than a foreign princess?"

Meira returned her father's smile, placing her free hand on top of his. In his own way, she knew her father was giving his approval. "Thank you, Father." Meira stood, pulling him up with her and into a hug. "I love you."

"I love you too, Meira," Lord Daesyn said as they

hugged. He pulled back and kissed her on the forehead before letting her go. "Now, go spend time with your prince."

* * *

Later that day, Meira found the castle far quieter than usual as she made her way to the tower to meet Gaelen, only to find it empty. No sign of him whatsoever, recently or otherwise, and on the bed, she found a book laying open—the same book Meira had bought at the bookshop and let Gaelen borrow. She sat on the edge of the bed before picking the book up and examining it. Flipping through, Meira paused when an illustration of a human with wings caught her attention. The passage next to the image spoke of fairies and how they could use magic to appear in different forms to humans, like the little balls of light she and Gaelen had seen in the oasis—among other interesting forms that beguiled the mind.

Meira waited for Gaelen for over an hour, but when he never arrived, she left the tower. She decided to see if she could find him. Perhaps he had been caught up in a political meeting or had fallen asleep and lost track of the time. Meira stepped into the garden, pausing as she realized the usual sounds of the garden workers no longer filled the air, and the area was enshrouded in an eerie silence.

Even the birds had stopped chirping.

Meira walked up the garden steps leading into the castle. None of the usual servants bustled around the hallways cleaning. Even the guards, usually stationed outside the throne room, were missing. Meira pushed the throne room doors open and entered, finding herself in darkness. What could have happened that all the candle chandeliers had been extinguished? She dashed out of the throne room, trying to think of where else Gaelen could be. She checked the library but found it empty, save for the books.

"Something's very wrong," she whispered, running back into the main hallway of the castle.

Meira dashed out of the castle and to the stables where her horse waited. Even the stable hands she'd seen that morning were gone.

Meira raced from the castle and back towards her house. Once she'd arrived at her house, she quickly dismounted Vala, handing the reins to the stablehand.

"My lady, is everything alright?" the stablehand asked.

Meira shook her head. "No, I . . . I need to see my father." She turned away, hurrying into the house. "Father!"

Meira entered the sitting room, expecting her father to be sitting in his chair by the fireplace again. Instead, she found it empty, save for the book he'd left open on the seat. Panic rose through her. Where was he? It made no sense for him not to be there—he wasn't supposed to leave for Hivale for a few more days.

Meira left the sitting room and turned down the hall, heading toward her father's study, where the door was cracked open. She pushed it open, breathing a sigh of relief. Her father sat hunched over a pile of parchment at his desk, an inked quill in hand. Haelyn sat in the chair opposite him, rambling about something or another. Her father seemed to mostly be ignoring her cousin, as usual when she came to him to gossip about what was going on at court.

"Father," Meira interrupted, walking over to the desk. "I need your help."

"Whatever it is, Meira, I'm sure it can wait. I was in the middle of telling your father about Lord Oran and me," Haelyn said.

Meira glared at Haelyn, her fingers clenching into a fist. She was beyond tired of her constant need for attention, even from her own uncle, and Meira had had enough. "Haelyn, I don't *care* about you and one of your many suitors, and I'm sure my father doesn't either. Something has happened, and I need to speak with my father about it *now*."

Haelyn stared at her, eyes wide and her mouth gaped open in shock. Blowing a puff of air out of her nostrils, she folded her arms across her chest.

Meira held eye contact with her for a long moment, unwavering and hoping she would grasp the point before she turned back to her father, forcing herself to unclench her fists.

Lord Daesyn had stood from his chair, ready to separate the two girls if needed. Seeing that they had both calmed down, he sat. "Meira, what is it? I thought you were meeting with Prince Gaelen?"

"I was, but he didn't show," Meira said. "I waited for over an hour, so I went looking for him. There's *no one* in the castle, Father. The servants, the guards, the queen, the prince. . . they're all gone. It's like they've completely disappeared."

Meira's father rubbed a wrinkled hand along his face, letting out a sigh. "Where did you check? Perhaps there was a meeting in the feast halls or somewhere you didn't look?"

"I searched the entire castle, and there's no trace of him, the queen, or *anyone*. And the throne room, Father. . . The throne room is filled with a terrible darkness. Something awful has happened," Meira answered. She stared at her father, pleading with him to recognize the seriousness of the situation.

Lord Daesyn studied his daughter intently for a few

moments then spoke in a grave tone. "Alright. I believe you, Meira, but what you're describing sounds like nothing I've ever heard of. I'll need to examine the situation at the castle myself. Let's go."

He stood from his chair and walked around the desk, pulling Meira into a hug. Meira took a shuddering breath as she leaned against him, breathing in the comforting and familiar scent of his robes.

"Everything will be alright, Meira. We'll get to the bottom of this as soon as we can," he reassured, rubbing a hand against her back.

Meira nodded, stepping away from him and starting to leave the room.

"Meira, wait…"

Meira turned to look at her cousin, whose arms were no longer folded across her chest. "I want to help you. Let me come."

Meira watched her cousin for a moment then nodded. "We should hurry."

* * *

Meira quickly changed out of her riding clothes and into a tunic and leggings. She then filled her quiver with arrows, pulling the strap over her shoulder once she'd finished.

Once they arrived, Meira first led her father into the throne room, while Haelyn checked the hallways and rooms of the castle, showing him the darkness that had been left behind. The throne room door stayed wide open, letting light in from the hallway so she and her father could see inside. As Meira stood in the center of the throne room, watching her father, a cold shiver ran down her spine as black shadows moved along the walls and floor.

"You're right, Meira. I've never seen anything like this," her father said. His boots echoed in the room as he walked. "What could have happened to them?"

Meira shook her head. "I don't know. But whatever it was must have been powerful if they were able to take the prince *and* the castle staff." It reminded her of a story she'd read when she was twelve, about a shadow fairy. She could manipulate shadows, molding them into different shapes —just like the ones moving along the walls.

"Let us go find Haelyn," her father suggested. He placed a comforting hand on her arm, leading her out and into the foyer where Haelyn waited.

"I searched every room and even went down into the creepy crypts. There's no sign of anyone," Haelyn said.

Meira's father shut the throne room door behind them, his brows furrowed together. He fidgeted with the sleeves of his robes and tucked his arms inside. Though she knew he was trying to hide his anxiety over the prince's and staff's disappearances, Meira could see it in his movements and eyes.

"I don't understand what could have happened," he said, his voice echoing in the foyer.

Haelyn looked skeptical. "There's no way the entire castle staff could just disappear without anyone noticing. What happened? Did fairies take them?" Haelyn suggested in a droll tone.

Meira's gaze snapped to her cousin, ready to lash out at her again, until she had a moment to process what she'd just said. "Of course," Meira whispered. She looked between her father and cousin, eyes wide with realization.

"Father, Haelyn. . . listen to me," she said. "This might sound crazy, but I think it's possible Prince Gaelen and the others have been taken by the fae. I'm going to find them."

"Meira, are you sure? Perhaps we should go with you?" her father asked, grabbing Meira's elbow as she turned to leave.

"Father, you know the stories of the fae almost as well as I do. All of the signs are there. I don't have time to explain why, but I need you to just trust me," Meira said.

"Meira. . . " Her father sighed.

Stepping forward, Meira quickly wrapped her arms around her father, pulling him into a tight hug. "Don't worry, Father. I'll be back as soon as I can, I promise."

Returning her hug, he nodded, pulling back after a moment. "Very well. Please, be careful, Meira."

Meira wrapped a hand around the strap of her quiver over her shoulder. "I will."

With that, Meira ran down the hall and to the entrance of the castle garden.

* * *

Something shifted in the air around her as Meira entered the castle garden once more. She slowed to what felt like a painstaking crawl, searching the garden as she walked along the stone path and her senses began tingling. After turning down several rows of the garden, she stopped on the pathway as she came face to face with the same blue lights. Some lit up the pathway on either side, while others flew around her in the air before moving farther down the path, as though they were trying to tell her *follow us.*

Meira considered the stories she'd read in books and what her father had long told her about the fae, trying to remember the different bits of lore. The fae were said to live in a world beyond her own, a world filled with ancient magic beyond even Meira's imagination. Their society held different rules and values than humans. Should Meira actually encounter a fae, she'd have to be careful of what she said.

The twinkling lights led her farther from the garden's center and toward the back corner opposite the tower, where a tall black oak tree stood. The tree's long branches created a yawning shadow, shrouding the corner in darkness, save for the lights that had stopped at the base of the tree.

Meira slowly approached, uncertain of whether she truly wanted to follow the tree's path. She didn't remember that particular tree ever being there before, and she and Gaelen had walked through the vast castle gardens many times in recent days.

She approached the tree with caution, unsure of what to expect. The small hairs along the back of her neck prickled as if she were being watched, more so than ever before. She wasn't alone. She looked around the area, turning slowly back toward the garden. Still empty. From behind, soft bells sounded again. It grew louder, almost as though someone chuckled right in her ear. She whirled around, only to find no one. Her brow furrowed, and she frowned at the empty space around her, which her instincts insisted was not as empty as it appeared to be.

Movement caught her eye. A human-sized figure popped out from behind the tree, leaning against the trunk with their arms folded over their chest. They had wild hair, partially covering slightly pointed ears. Their large eyes stared back at Meira as she realized what they were. Wings flapped behind them, a dead giveaway.

A fairy.

Meira darted down the path. The fairy laughed again, dancing around the tree's trunk before pausing again. Just as she came a few feet from the tree, the fairy disappeared. Meira stumbled to a stop, searching for any lingering sign of the fairy. An outline of a door appeared in the tree's bark, suggesting a doorway with a line of light.

Meira hesitated, not knowing what to expect if she dared to enter the tree. What would she find on the other side? Would she be able to return to the human world? What if it were a trap, and it wouldn't lead her to Gaelen at all? She steadied her breathing, pushing the doubts to the back of her mind.

If this was the only way for her to find Gaelen, she'd have to take her chances. Opening the door, Meira stepped inside, falling down into a black hole.

CHAPTER SIX

Meira screamed as she plummeted through the darkness, her hands grasping at air, desperate to find something—anything—to stop her plunge. She slammed into something hard, making her cry out as pain shot up her elbow and arm. Endlessly, she fell. Farther and farther, with no end in sight in the inky blackness. Her voice was rendered hoarse and raw, and she no longer *could* scream, but still she fell. Fear flowed through her. Where would this darkness lead her? Was there some horrible death waiting for her at the bottom? *Was* there a bottom?

Then, impact. What little wind was left in her lungs made an abrupt exit with an audible wheeze. Her arms and legs splayed out, pain radiating through her entire body. Focusing on her breathing, she slowly shifted around on the ground, moving her limbs carefully to make sure there were no injuries. Her hand moved along the ground, and the damp earth scraped under her nails.

Where was she? The air was cold, like she was in a cave or something. The smell of dirt filled her nostrils. Panic clawed through her as she sat up, her eyes trying to adjust to the darkness. Yet, she felt relief, her stomach finally having dropped from her throat, and her bow and quiver were undamaged. Lifting her throbbing head, she searched for any sign of light, but it was an exercise in futility.

Meira fought to control her breathing. *Panicking won't do me any good.* The sooner she took control of her surroundings, the sooner she could get out of here. Carefully standing, she held both arms out in front of her, feeling around for anything that might help. Her fingers met rough stone, and she moved her hand around, realizing it was a wall. Meira followed the wall, turning several times. She paused, considering the pattern of how many times she'd just turned.

She was in a maze. But without being able to see anything, how would she know if she was going the right way? She had to keep following the wall and hope she wouldn't run into a dead end—or worse, a trap. Meira knew she was traveling through uncharted territory, and the fae had the upper hand. Her father had told her stories of humans who'd fallen victims to the fae's tricks and how they'd returned from their world, but she wasn't sure her limited knowledge would be enough. Stories weren't real life.

Meira carefully moved away from the wall, holding her arms stretched out on both sides so she could feel around her as she walked. As she took a step, something on the ground caught the toe of her boot, and she fell forward, slamming hard into the ground, knocking the wind out of her. She cringed, squeezing her eyes tight as she fought to regain her breath. The throbbing of her knees kept her company all the while.

After forcing herself to her feet, she walked blind in the opposite direction, using her hands to feel along the wall. Finally, she stopped to catch her breath.

Meira closed her eyes, holding herself up against the wall. Was she out of her league, trying to fight her way through fae magic? What else would they have in store for her?

"Meira," a voice called. "Meira."

Meira held her breath. How could it have been this easy to have come all this way and found Gaelen already? Still, she would know his voice anywhere.

Meira looked away from the wall, heading toward Gaelen's voice. "Gaelen, where are you?" she called.

Turning the corner, she found Gaelen standing in front of a dead-end wall, with a bright light coming from behind him. Pushing her doubts to the back of her mind, she rushed toward him, relief washing over her.

"Gaelen, I've been so worried about you," Meira said, stopping a few feet in front of him.

"I'm fine, Meira," he said. "Meira, you need to go home and forget about me."

Meira frowned, shaking her head. "What are you talking about? Why would I forget about you? I came here to save you."

Gaelen stepped around and stopped behind her. "I don't need saving, Meira," he said. "My stepmother deserves the throne. I know that now."

Meira tracked his movement as he circled her, never taking her eyes off him, not believing a word he was saying. "What? Gaelen, you don't believe that."

"Yes, I do," he said. He stopped in front of her, making eye contact. "Besides, I like it here, in the fae lands. I've even found a fairy to marry."

"No. . . " Meira shook her head, blinking back tears. "I don't believe you."

"Meira, just go home. I don't love you. I never loved you. I'm going to give the throne to my stepmother."

"Gaelen, what are you saying? Why would you give up your throne to her?" she asked.

Gaelen turned his back to Meira, walking a few feet away. She rushed toward him, reaching out. Just as her fingers touched him, he faded.

Meira fell to her knees, lying back against the wall of the dead end. Exhausted tears tracked down her cheeks, and her breathing became ragged. "He wasn't real," she told herself forcefully. None of it was real.

Meira knew in her heart that Gaelen would never give in to his stepmother so easily, either, and it all had to be some kind of illusion created to mess with her mind.

She stood, feeling her way along the wall behind her until she came to a crack in the wall. Was this the only way out? She felt around inside the crack to gauge the opening before squeezing herself into it.

* * *

As soon as Meira wiggled into the wall's crack, she realized just how tight of a fit it was. She drew a tremoring breath, feeling the stone press up against her sternum. She carefully tried to raise her left arm, but the wall didn't give her much space to move. She could hardly breathe, much less move her legs.

Meira shifted, hoping if she turned her body, the walls would move enough for her to keep going, but they didn't budge. Panic surged through her once more as she realized she might well and truly be stuck.

Is this truly how I'm going to die? I'll never see Father again. I'll never ride my horse or see sunlight again, she thought. *I won't see Gaelen ever again. He'll be the queen's prisoner forever. I've failed him.*

The walls felt as though they were moving in on her. She gasped for air, arms burning as she fought to free them.

What would happen to the kingdom if Gaelen didn't escape the queen's grasp? She would claim the throne, and then what? What would happen to the people, to the land? Would they be turned into slaves? Would the shadows in the throne room slowly take over the entire castle, then the kingdom? What would happen to her father? Who would take care of him?

"No," Meira said. "I won't let that happen."

She closed her eyes and forced herself to focus, her breathing slowly leveling off as she eased into a normal pattern. As the effort of her breathing lessened, so did the pressure on her arms. Relief washed over her as she could move her chest and legs, and the walls moved farther away.

Meira squirmed farther inside the space between the walls, finding a room with a door. Curiously, there were lit candles all around the room, for which she was grateful. She wandered to the center of the room, taking her time to look around before approaching the door across the way. Meira turned the knob, hoping that by some chance it was unlocked, but no such luck.

She sighed and searched the room again. There had to be a way out of here, just as there had been with the walls. She combed over the area by the door more closely, noticing a strange looking mechanism above the door frame. Meira reached for her bow over her shoulder and nocked an arrow. Carefully aiming, she shot the mechanism. Gears creaked, and the door opened, allowing Meira to enter.

* * *

After everything the fae had already put Meira through, she didn't know what to expect on the other side of the door. Keeping her bow at the ready, she pushed the door open with a booted foot, peering into the room before entering. She looked around with a frown, realizing she was standing at the bottom of a spiral staircase. It soared upward through a maze of thorns, with no end in sight. She turned on the platform, searching for any other way out. The door behind her had disappeared, leaving a mockingly blank wall in its place.

With a deep breath, Meira replaced her bow and began mounting the steps, trudging on against the thorns as they caught on her pants and cloak, not unlike claws. Pain sparked at her scalp, forcing Meira to an abrupt halt— barbs, of course. She carefully pinned the loosened hair against her scalp with her fingertips and moved her head slowly from the thorn caught in her hair, clenching her teeth at its sharp grasp. Meira wasn't certain if the damp she felt in her hair was blood or sweat. Both were possible. Pausing on a landing halfway up the stairs, she stopped to catch her breath for a moment and give her aching thighs a rest. Looking up at the staircase, nothing had changed; all she saw was a maze of thorns and vines. She didn't know what she would find at the top of the staircase, but she hoped it wouldn't be an encore of downstairs.

Meira started climbing again, stepping over some of the lower vines that spilled across the steps. The vines caught on to her arms and legs like living creatures, and she winced as their sharp thorns stuck into her. She held her arms out to keep her balance as dizziness came over her, catching herself before she fell forward. Nearly kissing the stone step was still better than tumbling all the way back down, though.

Meira forged ahead, using the end of her bow to push a vine out of the way. Immediately, with such swiftness that it could only be magic, her world became a disorienting blur, and her stomach churned. Hugging herself and fighting the urge to gag, Meira's bruised knees found the stairs for support while she waited for the worst to pass. Meira knew she couldn't afford to waste time. Allowing herself a moment more, she stood back up and staggered up a few more steps before the bitter taste of bile urged her to stop again. When Meira looked up, she saw an image of herself with Gaelen, holding something wrapped in a blanket in her arms. A soft gasp escaped her before she could stop it. Was this a vision of the future or just another of the fae's tricks?

Her legs felt leaden at that point. Meira refused to give in to her growing weariness, lest she lean too much to one side and get pricked again. She just hoped that she'd be afforded a chance to rest between trials when she finally reached the top.

Meira looked around as a new but familiar scent drifted by her. She breathed it in, trying to place why it smelled so familiar, almost like pine, reminding her of being home, riding through the woods on her horse as the fragrance of juniper filled the air. The scent was strong, but there was no tree on the staircase. Unless it was hidden behind the impassable wall of thorns?

Meira remembered the sprig from the juniper tree Gaelen had given her—the same one she'd talked about with the queen. She closed her eyes, inhaling the scent as she concentrated and remembered her family's motto.

Strong of root, strong of thorn, she recited. Meira smiled, remembering the moment Gaelen had given it to her, and she knew she had to keep going.

Meira kept climbing and reached a second platform and looked down below her. The vines on the staircase below blocked her from seeing the ground she was so high up. She tilted her head back to take in what remained and withheld a sigh. There were many more stairs left to climb. She let out that breath, hoping she was finally near the end of this climb.

When she reached the last step, Meira fell forward onto the final platform, her breathing heavy. She leaned back onto her hands, looking up at the area above. A disturbingly pristine rope hung above her from a hole, as if it had been finished just yesterday, but there seemed to be no ceiling for the rope to hang *from*. She did not feel inclined to trust it, with or without fae trickery. Falling to her death because the rope gave out at an inopportune time was not on Meira's list of ideal ways to die. Given a chance to catch her breath, she stood and carefully took the rope in her hands, gently pulling on it. She was uncertain of whether she wanted to know where the rope would lead her. But what choice did she have? Her gaze wandered back down the staircase. It was covered in a maze of thorns and vines that only seemed to worsen the longer she stared at it, and she knew she'd never be able to make her way back down, even if she wanted to.

Giving the rope one more tug, she carefully wrapped it around both her arms and tugged again, using all her strength to pull herself up the rope.

Her arms felt as though they weighed a hundred pounds with each reach of the rope, feeling never ending. The rough texture burned against her palms as she held on tighter, climbing higher and higher and fighting not to lose her grip as increasingly raw hands began to sweat. She didn't dare look below or at her surroundings.

After what seemed like an age, Meira reached the top. With all the strength her arms could muster, she pulled herself up over the top of the rope.

CHAPTER SEVEN

Meira's upper body lay on the ground of a forest clearing, fighting the drag of her lower body still dangling in the hole as she grasped on to the edge. Using her last bit of strength, Meira pulled herself out. As soon as her legs were underneath her, the hole disappeared, replaced by the forest floor as though it had never been there. She drew a sharp breath, disoriented by the abrupt show of magic, but closed her eyes and once more steadied her breathing. Instead, she focused on the scent of the familiar forest around her, uncannily like the one she and Gaelen had picnicked in.

Meira opened her eyes again and forced herself to her feet before her body could lull her into a doze, wiping the dirt off her pants. As she stood to her full height, she looked ahead of her and gasped. Leaning against a tree several feet in front of her, their arms crossed over their chest, was the same fae she'd seen in the castle garden. Their wild hair blew in the soft breeze, their eyes wide and never leaving hers.

"Who are you?" the fairy asked.

Meira took a few steps forward, keeping her eyes on the fae. Remembering the stories her father had told her, she knew not to give her name. Fae took names very seriously and would use hers against her given the chance. "Someone seeking to help her prince," she said.

The fairy regarded Meira carefully, an almost skeptical look coming over their face. Meira took another step forward. The fairy wore a dress made from a single green flower petal, like an oversized dianthus blossom, with arm and leg slits cut into it and her wings flapping behind her.

"Hm," the fairy said. She reached into a pouch hanging from a belt at her waist and pulled a small cake out, bringing it to her lips. Pausing, she raised her eyes to Meira as she held the cake out. "Are you hungry?"

Meira thought of her grumbling stomach. When was the last time she'd eaten anything? She chewed on the inside of her lip, hoping that she didn't draw blood from her hunger with the nervous habit. The temptation was strong, but she knew better than to accept food from fairies. Even one little bite could be too much, according to the stories she'd read, and might be just enough to trap her in the fae lands forever.

"No, thank you," she said with a shake of her head. "I just want to find my prince."

"Are you sure that's what you really want?" the fairy asked, raising an eyebrow. "Are you sure there's nothing more? No jewels?" She took another bite of cake.

"No. I just want to help my prince," Meira repeated.

The fairy took one last bite of cake, polishing it off, then wiped any crumbs from her hands. She moved away from the tree and started walking away before pausing, looking back over her shoulder. "Follow me."

Meira tilted her head as she watched the fairy for a

moment, uncertain of whether she really should follow. The fairy seemed friendly enough, but even friendly fairies weren't without their games. Meira ultimately stayed a few feet behind as she followed, not wanting to lose her trail. All the while, she watched her surroundings, looking for any sign of mushroom rings—a sure sign of fairy rings in disguise, used to trap humans.

The fairy led Meira to a large clearing, pausing at the edge. Fae of all kinds surrounded the clearing, some hanging from tree branches while others flew around on wings of different shapes and colors. Sprites no bigger than Meira's palm spun around high in the air, clasping each other's tiny hands as they lowered themselves to her height to inspect their guest. A fairy standing nearby had long feathery arms and a sort of net in her hair with jewels and a pear inside the net. The jewels seemed to almost glow, which Meira found fascinating.

The fae court was everything she'd ever imagined it to be. As she looked around the clearing, her eyes paused on a woman standing in its center. Long dark hair fell against her back in a cacophony of twists and braids beneath a crown of golden leaves, with a matching dress flowing down to the ground, its long sleeves loose. Behind her sat a leaf-shaped throne.

The fairy who'd led Meira to the clearing approached the woman, bowing her head. "Queen Lythienne of the Woodland Court, may I present the human girl who is searching for her prince?"

Meira forced herself not to shrink back as the queen's eyes met hers. Keeping her arms at her sides, Meira bowed. Unlike Queen Averith, this queen at least seemed a little more friendly and didn't give Meira any instant shivers running down her spine. She hoped that friendly feeling would continue.

"What gives this human the right to enter my court?" the queen asked.

"I have tested the girl's knowledge of our world, and she passed, Your Majesty," the fairy said. "She is searching for her prince and entered our world knowing what dangers she may be presented with."

"That's hardly enough reason to allow her into my court without an invitation." The queen sneered. She turned and sat on the leaf throne, resting an elbow on its armrest and cupping her chin. "Still, you must be very brave and determined to have endured all that you did in the maze. You will need that bravery if you wish to save your prince."

"That's all I want, Your Majesty," Meira said.

"You must be exhausted after your journey, so you have my permission to stay the night," the queen said. "What name may we call you by?"

"Eirian," Meira answered, keeping the laws of the fae in mind. Saying the name out loud stung, solidifying that her sister was, in fact, gone, and that she was truly taking her place at court and in life. But what harm could it do? Her sister was already dead. She didn't know if using her sister's name would lead to any repercussions should the fae queen find out, but it was already too late.

"I welcome you to my court, Eirian," the queen said. "My courtier, Poppy, will show you where you may rest. But first, may I offer you something to eat? You must be famished after your journey."

The queen waved a hand, and a purple swirl of magic moved through the air and into the center of the clearing. As it faded, a long wooden table appeared, laid out with a colorful spread of food—cakes, breads, drinks, and more, enough to feed a whole army.

Meira's stomach grumbled again, this time louder than before. She *was* famished, and she knew she couldn't resist eating something for much longer. It was one thing to refuse the courtier who had brought Meira to the queen to begin with, but to potentially offend the queen was another matter entirely.

"I don't blame you for your hesitation, Eirian," the queen said after a moment. "It's clear you really do know much about our ways. Therefore, I promise you here, in front of my court as witness, that consuming anything from the food spread before you nor anywhere else will not endanger you in any way, nor will you be trapped in our lands."

Meira watched the queen for a moment, considering her words. *Do I dare believe her?* She turned toward the spread of food, her tongue sweeping her lips as the aroma of warm breads entered her nostrils. She thought back to the myths and legends book in her father's book collection, remembering a story about a human who'd wandered too far into fae territory. The human encountered a fae, who offered them a piece of bread, after promising that no harm would come to them.

"Perhaps I could eat just a little something, then," Meira said.

The queen nodded, gesturing toward the table. "Please, eat as much as you wish."

Meira stepped toward the table, observing the spread of food. She picked up a cake no bigger than her palm, covered with lavender icing, and took a bite—and the taste matched what she imagined the flower itself might taste like, curiously enough. She finished the cake then took a bite of bread and a sip of a sweet purple liquid.

After eating one more cake, Meira looked up at the queen, who watched her with an amused smile. Meira stepped away from the table, glad to have finally eaten.

"Your Majesty, if I may, I'd like to ask a question," she said.

"Certainly, my dear," Queen Lythienne said.

"I believe the queen regent of my kingdom may somehow be involved with my prince's disappearance," Meira said. "When I went to the castle, both she and the prince had vanished, as had the servants. Do you have any idea how that might have happened?"

The queen considered Meira's question for a moment. "I do not know for certain. It's possible that she is involved," she said. "But, it is getting late, and I'm sure you are exhausted from your journey. We shall speak more on this tomorrow, when you've had a chance to sleep."

Meira frowned. She didn't want to wait; she wanted to know more about what had happened to Gaelen and the castle workers. But she couldn't argue that she *wasn't* tired without lying to the queen's face, so she decided not to, knowing morning would arrive soon enough, and she could ask more questions then.

CHAPTER EIGHT

Meira followed Poppy, the fairy who had led her into Queen Lythienne's court, to the edge of the clearing where a tent had been set up for her. Several small lit lanterns hung above the tent on one of the branches.

"This is where you may rest for the night, Lady Eirian," Poppy said. "Queen Lythienne will call upon you in the morning."

"Thank you," Meira said.

Poppy bowed her head as her purple wings lifted her off the ground and into the air, flying back toward Queen Lythienne's throne.

Meira entered the tent, where she found a neatly folded pile of fresh clothing, including a nightgown, had been laid on top of a bedroll. The thought of sleeping on the ground was strange to her, having never done it before, but she was grateful to at least be given some privacy within the tent.

After placing her quiver and bow next to the bedroll, Meira gently began to pull at her clothing, grimacing with every movement of her aching arms and legs. She'd be glad to be lying down soon enough, though she doubted the soreness in her aching body would stop immediately. Glad to be rid of the sweat and dirt-encrusted clothes she'd been wearing, she pulled the nightgown over her.

Meira's mind raced as she lay on the bedroll, unable to sleep. What kind of obstacles could Queen Averith throw at her if she knew she was trying to find Gaelen?

She pulled her legs up to her chest, wrapping her arms around them as she rested her chin on her knee, thinking about what she would do the following day.

If I'm going to gain Queen Lythienne's trust and get help from her, I need to do whatever I can to stay on her good side.

With a frustrated sigh, Meira got up and walked out of the tent, looking around the clearing. Up ahead, fairy creatures gathered around the campfire near the center, not far from the queen's throne, though the queen herself had vanished.

Meira reached up, removing one of the lanterns from the branch hanging above. Using the lantern to light her way, she wandered away from the clearing. She made her way down a path and stopped near the edge of a small lake, where the treetops of the forest had broken, allowing the moonlight to shine down into the water.

A figure stood bent over the water's edge, dipping a bucket into the impossibly clear water. Meira paused several feet back from the lake, not wanting to frighten them. The figure stood back up, pulling the bucket of water to their chest and turning toward Meira. They looked like an owl, with feathered arms and a rounded face, their eyes large and yellow.

"Oh!" the figure cried, startled. He jumped back, nearly plunging into the crisp water but catching himself at the last moment. "Who are you, and what are you doing here?"

"I couldn't sleep and was just taking a walk. I didn't mean to disturb you," Meira said.

The fae regarded her, skeptical, and pulled the bucket close to his chest. "That's all right. I was just collecting water for the Court of Shells ambassador. I didn't expect anyone else to come to the lake," he said.

Meira looked behind the fae, noticing a pile of empty buckets by the water's edge. Perhaps if she befriended this fae, or one of the other members of the court, she could ask them to call her Fae Friend. From what she remembered of the lore she'd read, if a fae agreed to be a human's Fae Friend, they would owe the human a debt, which Meira could leverage to her advantage while at court.

"Do you have to carry more than one load of water back and forth?" she asked after a moment.

He nodded, clicking his beak together. "Yes, but these are the last four, luckily. At least until tomorrow, when the ambassador inevitably complains again."

"Would you like some help?" Meira asked.

The owl fae gave her a surprised look, as though not expecting Meira to offer help. "I would appreciate that, thank you."

Meira passed the fairy and moved toward the pile of buckets, taking one in each hand and moving to the water's edge. Kneeling down, she scooped the water into each bucket before straightening. She tried to maintain her balance as she lifted each bucket, suddenly realizing just how heavy they both were.

Meira waddled carefully after the fairy and followed beside him along the path, heading back to the clearing. "What does the ambassador need the water for?"

"His underwater suite," he said. "The quality isn't good enough for him, apparently. He refuses to enter into a trade with Queen Lythienne until he is satisfied, which means I could be gathering many more buckets of water for the next week."

Meira chewed on her lip, listening to the owl. "What would help make the quality of the water better?"

"Apparently the ambassador is used to fresher water and says that pearls are the best way to clean it and give it a more natural quality," the fairy answered. "He came here with a supply of them for his stay, but the last pearl was stolen out of his room. Personally, I think he's just being stubborn and trying to keep us distracted so he can prolong the trade agreement."

Meira raised an eyebrow at the owl's last comment but said nothing. As they reached the clearing, she looked over to where she'd abandoned her bedroll. On one hand, part of her wanted to part ways with the owl for the night and go to sleep. But on the other hand, the curious part of her wanted to push onward and see what happened with the ambassador.

The owl led her farther into the clearing, following another pathway until they reached the base of the tree towering behind Queen Lythienne's throne, looking as though it might reach the stars themselves. Its branches lit up like the night sky. Meira stared up at it in awe, for a moment forgetting the weight pulling down on her shoulders, watching as tiny balls of lights floated around from branch to branch, fluttering through the sky.

"Is this where the queen lives?" she asked.

"It is. All members of the court live in the tree with the queen, and it is where the ambassador is staying," the owl said. "We should hurry, however. It's getting late, and you'll want to get plenty of sleep."

A tiny door appeared within the tree's base, coming up to Meira's knees.

"But. . . how will I possibly fit through the door?" Meira asked.

"Do not worry. The court's magic will allow you to enter and exit the tree as though you were the right size," he replied, stepping inside the tree.

Meira's eyes widened as she watched the owl disappear into the tree. After a moment she followed, finding herself in a large room resembling a foyer, with hallways straight ahead and to both sides of her.

"Come, come," the owl beckoned.

They walked down the hall and turned a corner, then walked several feet before pausing at a wooden door. "If you place the buckets down here, I can do the rest and make sure the ambassador is satisfied with the water," the owl said. "I owe you a debt for helping me carry these buckets. I am Garvan. Should you ever need my help while you are here, please do not hesitate to ask me."

Meira bowed her head. "I will bear that in mind," she said, placing the buckets down. "Goodnight, Garvan."

Meira walked back down the hallway and toward the tree's entrance, heading back to her tent. The queen's issue with the ambassador intrigued her, and she wondered if she could use it to her advantage somehow. Asking the ambassador to claim her as a Fae Friend wouldn't be enough—he'd want something in return, which meant finding a pearl. Where could she find a pearl that would satisfy the ambassador?

Mother's necklace.

After arriving back at her tent, Meira knelt by the bedroll. She reached up and unclasped the necklace she'd worn at the ball around her neck, holding it in her palm as she examined it.

Could she really give up her mother's necklace to the ambassador? Besides a few books, it was among her mother's most valuable possessions, said to be a family heirloom passed down through generations. Originally passed on to Eirian, she still remembered the day her sister had given it to her, when she was still too ill to get out of bed. *Mother would want you to have it.*

Taking a deep breath, she reached up and clipped the chain around her neck, letting the pearl fall to her chest one last time to feel the familiar, subtle weight. Standing again, Meira walked back toward the tree, entering and wandering down several hallways, until she finally found the chamber. Part of her wanted to turn back and think of another way. *Father would be furious*, she thought. *No. . . I have to do this.*

Pausing in front of the door and knocking, she hoped she wasn't making a mistake. A muffled voice answered the knock, and the door opened after a moment, revealing a fairy with gills on each side of its face, its hands and feet webbed. He stared at Meira with large black eyes with nostrils between them.

"Who are you? What do you want?" the ambassador hissed.

"I . . ." Meira swallowed. Perhaps she hadn't thought this through completely. "I was speaking to Garvan, and he mentioned that a pearl would be useful in helping with the quality of your water, and I'm here to bring one to you. But first, I have a favor to ask."

The ambassador regarded her carefully. "And who are you to ask me for a favor?" he asked, his words almost a whisper.

"Who I am is of no concern to you. The favor I would ask is for your support in asking Queen Lythienne for me to be a Friend of the Fae tomorrow," Meira answered.

Taking a deep breath, she reached up to unclasp her necklace, carefully placing it in her palm. She looked longingly at the pearl one last time, as though she were saying goodbye to an old friend.

For Gaelen, she thought, holding the necklace out toward the ambassador. "The pearl is yours, if you will grant me this favor."

A long, forked tongue poked out between two pointed teeth as the fairy stared down at the pearl in Meira's hand. "That pearl *is* quite large," he said. "Where did you get such a fine specimen?"

Meira swallowed hard, almost not wanting to give an answer. "It was my mother's," she said after a moment, shaking her head. "It's yours, if you so desire."

The fairy made a thoughtful "hm" sound, his forked tongue poking out from his mouth again. "It would certainly help with the quality of my water." He looked down at her. "I accept your offer. Tomorrow, at court, I will step forward and support your claim to be a Fae Friend."

Meira held the pearl out farther, holding her gaze on it one last time. The fairy reached his webbed hands out, yanking the pearl from hers. He raised it to his flat nose, sniffing it. "I thank you for getting this for me. Now, I shall retire."

The fairy stepped back and closed the door behind him. Meira let out a sigh of relief, closing her eyes for a moment. Had she made the right decision? What would her father think of her giving up her mother's most prized possession? Would he agree it was worth the cost to restore the rightful heir to the throne? For her own future, if she dared to venture it?

It's too late now, she thought. She just had to hope everything would go smoothly at court the next day.

* * *

Meira stood at the back of the clearing under the tree where her tent was set up, watching as members of the queen's court began gathering. Queen Lythienne's leaf-shaped throne sat empty. Courtiers flew around the clearing, some retreating into the treetops and others staying at the clearing's edge.

Tiny fairies no bigger than her palm danced in the clearing's center, playing music on tiny flutes and dancing in tune to their song. As the music died down, a purple cloud of smoke enveloped the throne. The smoke disappeared after a moment, revealing Queen Lythienne sitting on her throne.

"Where is the human girl Eirian?" Queen Lythienne asked.

Meira looked around as members of the queen's court turned toward her. Panic rose in her throat as she stepped forward, walking through the center of the clearing and pausing a few feet away from the queen.

"Ambassador Ginko tells me you two spoke last night," the queen said.

Meira's heart pounded in her chest. "We did, Your Majesty," Meira said. "I am thankful for the hospitality you have shown me thus far. I hope for that hospitality to continue while I am here in your courts and lands, and I have asked Ambassador Ginko to support me in what I am about to ask of you."

Meira paused, watching the crowd around her before looking back at the queen, who watched with a raised eyebrow. "Go on," she said.

"I was unable to sleep last night, and I overheard a lot of conversations going on. When I spoke with the ambassador, we came to an arrangement," Meira continued. "I ask for you to name me Friend of the Fae, and for the right to petition for aid as a courtier."

Meira swallowed hard, hoping she hadn't just made a terrible mistake, but Queen Lythienne showed no outward sign of anger.

"I see," the queen said. Her eyes searched the clearing. "Ambassador Ginko, where are you?"

Meira turned, looking for any sign of the ambassador, hoping he would follow through with his promise. After a moment, he stepped forward through the crowd.

"I am here, Your Majesty," the ambassador said with a bow. "It is true what the human says, and I support her claim to be Friend of the Fae."

Queen Lythienne raised an eyebrow. "Oh? And what has this girl offered to make you support such a claim?"

Ambassador Ginko pulled the pearl necklace from a pouch on his belt. "She offered me this magnificent pearl, so that I may use it during my stay here. I look forward to finalizing negotiations with you, Queen Lythienne."

"Where did you get such a pearl, Eirian?" the queen asked.

Meira smiled sadly. "It was my mother's."

The queen raised an eyebrow in surprise. "Giving such a prized possession to the ambassador is quite a sacrifice for you to make. Are you sure this is what you want?"

Meira blinked back the hot burn of tears that sprang

unbidden to her eyes. "It doesn't matter. I just want to help my prince."

Queen Lythienne shifted, resting her arm on the throne's armrest. "It seems you do, indeed, know much about our laws, human," she said. "I have been waiting a long time for someone with your knowledge to come to our lands—someone who, perhaps, could help reunite our lands once more, and I could name Friend of the Fae. Tell us more about the help you seek."

Meira took a deep breath, looking around the clearing at the different court members before turning her gaze back to the queen. "Prince Gaelen, the rightful king to the human kingdom of Alythia, and I are childhood sweethearts. A few days ago, I thought I saw Poppy in the castle garden, but I wasn't sure. Before I came here, I discovered that Gaelen, along with all of the castle staff and the queen regent, had disappeared from the castle. I remembered the tales my father told me as a child. He told me of ancient, wise beings who roamed the earth and sometimes crossed the barrier between our realms. He even told me that at one time, our people co-existed amongst each other, and the kingdoms were once allies."

Looking around, Meira saw no sign of any offense being taken by what she'd said so far. "I've walked through a maze that I nearly lost myself in. I was pricked by thorns that caused me to hallucinate. I will do whatever I need to find my prince. . . but I cannot do it on my own. I need your help."

"Hm," Queen Lythienne said thoughtfully. She rested her elbow on the armrest of the throne, using her hand to rest her chin in her palm. "It seems to me that there is only one way to know for sure whether your prince is here in the fae lands, and where he is located," she said.

The queen stood and strode to the center of the clearing. She stretched a hand out into the air, murmuring something incoherent from where Meira watched. Long purple tendrils shot out of her fingers, creating a dark purple circle in the air. In the circle, a cloud of smoke slowly disappeared, revealing a tower surrounded by a maze of thorns and bushes. The clouds above the tower were dark and gray, with not an inch of sunlight peeking out.

Gaelen sat perched on the sill of the tower's window, leaning against the wall as he looked out into the distance, his eyes sad.

Meira gasped, rushing toward the circle. "Gaelen," she whispered, her heart pounding. She turned toward the queen. "Do you know where that tower is? Who is holding him prisoner?"

Queen Lythienne nodded, turning toward her with a grim look on her features. "Yes, I know where it is," she said. "He is in the Shadowlands, being held prisoner by Queen Averith."

"Queen Averith?" Meira asked. "That's Gaelen's stepmother..."

Meira thought back to that moment in the garden when she'd seen the queen's reflection change in the water. "Is Queen Averith a fairy?"

"Yes, she is the queen of the Shadowlands," Queen Lythienne said. "Many of our kind have been captured by her and turned into shadow creatures, never to be seen or heard from again."

The pieces began to coalesce in Meira's mind, remembering what Gaelen had said about the marriage law. If Averith could pressure Gaelen into sharing that power, she would be able to keep her claim to the throne while keeping control over Gaelen. She would rule both the Shadowlands and the human kingdom.

"Unfortunately, Queen Lythienne and the other fae courts are not allowed to interfere with Queen Averith's affairs due to an old treaty," one of the courtiers said.

Queen Lythienne nodded. "That is correct. But if she's removed from power, it would be beneficial to both my court and the other fae who've been taken as her shadow slaves." She turned toward the crowd of courtiers. "Who will step forward to help Eirian free the prince from Queen Averith?"

Silence. Meira looked around the clearing as members of the court whispered to each other, and she thought for sure she'd have to continue her journey on her own.

She heard Garvan's deep voice call. "I will help Eirian." The owl stepped forward, bowing his head to Lythienne. "She was kind enough to help me with the ambassador's needs last night."

"So will I," another voice called. Meira turned, surprised to see Poppy step forward. She looked at Meira, bowing her head. "I will do whatever I can to help you on your journey."

CHAPTER NINE

Images of Gaelen trapped in the queen's tower plagued Meira's mind, refusing her any hope of sleep. She sat up on her bedroll, arms loosely clasped around her knees as she waited for the sun to rise. When daybreak graced the clearing, Meira groggily left the tent, pulling her cloak around her as she wandered.

Before long, Meira found Queen Lythienne walking through the forest with a pair of courtiers. Shaking away her lingering drowsiness, she forced herself to focus on the present, knowing that she needed to at least try to be presentable. She approached cautiously, waiting until Queen Lythienne made eye contact with her before moving closer.

"Will you excuse me, gentlemen?" the queen asked, turning toward Meira with a soft smile. The courtiers bowed and walked away as Lythienne gestured for Meira to come closer. "Come walk with me, Eirian."

Meira bowed her head and did as the queen asked, walking next to her. She wanted so much to ask a barrage of questions about the coming expedition but knew she was better off being patient.

"Your journey to the Shadowlands will begin soon," she said. "There are some things you should know, however, and one thing you must do before you can begin. You must find an amber gemstone and pull it from the heart of a living tree. You can find the tree within the forest, in a swampy region called Mistwood. Should you find the gemstone, it may prove useful against Queen Averith."

Meira hesitated, thinking back to what she had already endured in the maze. Would she be able to endure another of the fae's tests? Unfortunately, she knew she didn't have a choice. *If I succeed, it will bring me one step closer to finding and rescuing Gaelen.*

Lythienne led Meira through the forest, bringing her farther and farther from the clearing. After a few minutes of walking, she paused at the edge of a clear path. Straight ahead, Meira saw a dark and swampy area, filled with trees and moss.

"This is the edge of my territory, and as far as I can bring you," Lythienne said. "You must leave your bow and arrows behind, and you must go alone."

Meira stared out into the swamp, trying to glimpse what—or whom—she might run into, but all she saw were trees, grass, mud, and gleams of water. She reached over her shoulder and pulled her bow off, placing it carefully by a nearby tree before pulling her quiver of arrows off. Her fingers touched the juniper tree pin she'd pinned to the strap, and she smiled. If she couldn't bring her arrows with her, she could at least take that. She carefully unpinned it from the strap and transferred it to the left breast of her shirt.

Taking a deep breath, Meira stepped onto the spongy,

wet earth of a path leading deeper into the swamp. The ground became softer the deeper she went until it began to suck at her boots, pulling them deeper with every step.

Stopping to study the ground, she realized it was barely solid. Her feet sank farther as she stood, trying to think fast. The mud was settling around her ankles and entirely covered the toes of her boots.

I'm going to sink to my hips if I don't get out of this mud soon, she thought as she looked around the swamp. A few steps away, a large crooked tree stood settled over a mound of grassy earth and knotted roots. Meira struggled to free her boots and found the tree's roots provided a far more reliable path than the subsuming earth, and the swamp-land was dense with woody pillars at her disposal.

Keeping her arms out wide for balance, Meira began navigating her new path, picking her way across dense roots and jumping from one set to another to avoid the hungry ground. Just as she was starting to feel a little more comfortable with her new route, her foot slipped off a particularly wet root. Her arms flailed as she tried to keep herself from falling, lurching toward a nearby tree branch and snatching the gnarled wood.

Meira took a deep breath, still clutching the branch as she looked around the swamp. How much farther would she have to go before finding the tree she was looking for?

All around her, the swamp seemed to hold fewer trees and more mud, almost as if the soupy earth was rising up, trying to pursue her as she carefully navigated the tree-root path. She jumped onto a nearby log and breathed a sigh of relief that the wood wasn't too rotten to bear her weight. Carefully, she walked along its mossy length to the far end.

A low rumbling sound sent her gaze sweeping around the swamp, searching for a source, and seeing only trees as the mud began to stir. The small hairs on the back of her neck rose, sending a shiver down her spine. The mud swirled sluggishly, and the rumbling sound swelled into a furious growl. A figure of mud burst forth from the increasingly churning, soggy ground. Droplets of brackish water struck Meira's face as the thing towered over her.

Meira screamed, lost her balance in a panicked retreat, and fell into the flowing mud. It swallowed her whole, and for a moment her world was a cold, wet, suffocating sludge. She kicked upward and gasped when her head broke the surface, and struggled to swim through the muck, desperate to reach a nearby log that offered escape, and she scrambled onto it.

Covered in oozing black mud, she faced the towering monster. It wasn't entirely made of mud. Long vines hung from it, twisting over and around its body, and odd twigs stuck out seemingly at random from its mud-flesh. Meira's stomach churned when she noticed a dead fish tail sticking out of its shoulder.

"Who are you?" the figure demanded, his voice deep.

Meira took a slow, deep breath, wrapping her arms around the log as she looked up at the creature. "My name is Meira. I was sent here by Queen Lythienne."

"And why would she send *you* into my swamp?" the mud creature asked.

"I've been chosen to recover something from the swamp. Something I need in order to save my prince, who has been imprisoned by the queen of the Shadowlands."

The mud creature roared again, jumping out of the mud and onto a nearby mound. "Chosen you may be, but none unworthy shall go near the tree!"

The mud creature charged towards Meira, its massive frame causing the ground to tremble with each thunderous step. She could feel the weight of it in her chest as she frantically leaped from one unstable mound to the other, her heart racing in terror.

But no matter how far she ran, the monster seemed to gain on her, its long arms reaching out with deadly intent. Meira's breath came in ragged gasps as she pushed herself deeper into the murky swamp, her feet sinking into the mire and slowing her down.

She knew she had to reach the tree—it was her only chance of survival. With every passing moment, the creature drew closer, its dark form darting through the tangled trees like a relentless predator.

Meira walked her body forward, fighting against the thick mud that threatened to swallow her whole. She risked a glance over her shoulder and saw the creature bearing down on her, its grotesque features twisted into a snarl of hunger. The sound of its heavy breathing and thudding footsteps echoed in her ears, spurring her onward.

Meira turned back, looking for another mound to jump to, only to realize there were none. Knowing she had no choice, she jumped into the waist-high water.

Meira expected her feet to immediately find the bottom beneath the surface, but they didn't. Her body sank fast, sucking the air from her lungs. Meira thrashed beneath the murky water, trying to readjust her eyes as it stung at them, trying to swim. Rising through to the surface, she gasped for breath, strands of hair loosening from her braid and sticking to her skin.

Meira looked over her shoulder and spotted the monster, but he clearly couldn't see her.

"You can't hide from me!" the monster bellowed.

Taking a deep breath, Meira dove into the water again, swimming farther away. After a few minutes, she came up for air a few feet from land. She moved through the water, crawling out onto the outer banks of a tree island.

Meira's body begged her to stop and rest. *No, I have to keep going*, she told herself. Using a nearby tree to pull herself up from the bank, she scurried through the trees quietly.

The monster's growls echoed in the distance, sounding farther and farther away. "You can't run, either!"

Meira stopped beside a cypress tree. Rubbing the ribbed bark, she searched for any sign that it was the correct tree. Finding none, she moved on to the next. Finally, she touched the last tree and realized none of them were the right one and growled in frustration. Behind her, the monster let loose another echoing growl. She turned in the mud, continuing to trudge through it.

Meira reached the end of her current leg of the swampy struggle, climbing out of the mud and flopping gracelessly onto a dirt path, her breathing heavy. A rising fog filtered through the swamp in front of her, blotting out her path.

The monster let out another rumbling growl, audibly closer, and Meira's heart raced. Holding her arms out, she found a tree and moved behind it, listening for the monster's footsteps. *If he can't find me, maybe he'll stop searching for me and return to the tree.*

Meira held her breath, tucking herself tightly against the tree. Her fingers brushed along the rough trees as the shadow of the mud monster appeared on the trunk of a nearby tree. His heavy panting filled the air. He walked farther away, and she released the breath she'd been holding. Peeking around the tree, she saw no sign of the creature.

Treading carefully, Meira stepped out from behind her shelter, fog swirling in her wake. Her shakes subsided with several deep breaths, focusing on banishing the fear that had crept up on her. The fog dissipated like spun sugar dipped in water, revealing a long, winding dirt path leading toward a gnarled, ugly tree in the distance. The tightness in Meira's chest lightened. *That has to be it.*

Meira's soaking pants weighed her steps as she passed through the knee-high grass growing between the trees. The tree was even homelier up close, with wart-like protrusions sprouting from branches thicker than her torso. Off-color ooze seeped from them, the deep orange saying stay away.

The illusion of plagued bulbs faded as she moved closer, leaving an ancient, gnarled tree with branches that spread across the width of the meadow, shadowing her from the cloud-veiled sunlight. Closing the distance between her and the tree, Meira immediately noticed the hollow in the center of its trunk.

She reached into the hollow, her fingers eagerly searching for what she hoped might be in there. The rough bark grew into soft moss, and then she felt it. Carefully wrapping her fingers around it, she pulled her arm back, revealing the amber stone. Even though the sunlight was blocked by the tree's branches, the gemstone glimmered in her hand, and Meira breathed a sigh of relief.

Behind her, a loud growl tore through the swamp, and she sucked in a sharp breath, clutching the stone to her chest. He rushed at her, grabbing at her legs. Meira screamed, her stomach plummeting as she started climbing up the tree's trunk. Holding tight to the stone in one hand, she pulled herself up into the tree. Bark shredded under her nails as she clawed her way up the broad trunk. Wind whistled past her ankle as the monster swiped at her, and gathering her strength, she leaped for a low branch.

Meira pulled herself onto the branch, breathing heavily as she looked down upon the monster from her precarious perch. The monster jumped up, stretching his long muddy arms out as far as he could to try and reach her.

"That stone is mine!" he howled.

Meira looked down at the stone again. Clearly, there was a specific reason the queen wanted her to find it, and a reason the monster was guarding it. It was warm in her palm, and light sparkled in its depths. Meira peered closer, and the stone grew hot in her palm. A sense of restrained power radiated from it.

The monster snatched at her, yanking her down out of the tree by her ankle. Meira screamed and fumbled the stone, nearly dropping it. She managed to catch it before it slipped away, but the monster reached for her again at the same moment. The feeling of power flared as the stone pointed toward the monster as its fingers closed over her wrist, and light erupted outward. The monster howled and released her, the cold slime of his touch at odds with the comforting warmth in her palm. The monster paced below her, and she turned the stone toward it.

The monster grew still. He peered up at Meira, the mud sloughing off to reveal a man's face beneath. There was no mistaking the look of relief in his green eyes.

"Meira, you are worthy of Amiroth's Sun Stone," he said.

Meira looked at the stone. "Is that what it's called?"

The man gave a grimacing grin. "Yes. Gods, I've been guarding it for so long, both our names have been forgotten, haven't they?"

Meira gave a slow nod. "What is your name?"

He shook his head. "It doesn't matter. What matters

now is that I can finally rest." The man gave a kind smile as he faded away before her.

Meira stayed rooted in place, attempting to make heads or tails of what had just happened. So many questions swirled through her mind as she tried to put the pieces together. She looked down at the stone still lightly glowing in her hands then placed it carefully into her pouch before climbing the rest of the way down.

She breathed a sigh of relief as her feet once more met solid earth. It was time to return to Queen Lythienne's court.

* * *

Meira arrived in Queen Lythienne's court a short time later, exhausted and still cold and wet. Queen Lythienne perched on her throne as Meira entered the clearing, a pleased smile crossing her features.

"Ah, Eirian, you have returned," the queen said. "I trust you were successful?"

Meira nodded, uncertain. Although it seemed like the man had been at peace, she couldn't shake her guilt over the part she had played in his fate.

"I was, Your Majesty," she said. "Though, I could do with a bath." Carefully reaching into her pouch, she pulled the stone out and stepped forward, presenting it to the queen.

The queen smiled. "Well, we can certainly arrange for that," she said. "You have passed the final test and shown that you are worthy of being named Fae Friend."

Meira took a deep breath, returning the queen's smile.

"There is no sunlight in the Shadowlands," the queen continued. "And Queen Averith has shadow creatures that do her bidding, so you will need something that will work against them and the queen, which is where the stone comes in." She gestured toward one of the courtiers, who stepped forward, handing over Meira's bow and quiver. Meira quickly took them from the courtier, glad to have them back.

Meira took in a deep breath, gazing up at the forest canopy as small lights of many colors moved through the trees.

"Your Majesty, before I came here, I saw tiny little lights in the prince's garden and then in the oasis. Were they fairies?" Meira asked, pointing up.

Queen Lythienne nodded. "Yes, those are my sprites. I received word that the prince was in the Shadowlands, so I sent them into the prince's garden as a way to lure you here." She gestured for Meira to follow, moving away from the throne. "I have to say, I'm quite impressed with how far you've come and with your knowledge of our ways."

"Thank you, Your Majesty. I do admit that I am a little fuzzy on what the Fae Friend law gives protection to. Does it include true names in its protection?" Meira asked.

The queen turned toward her and nodded. "It does. Why do you ask?"

Meira hesitated, wondering if she wanted to reveal the truth about the name she'd given the queen or if she should keep it to herself. It felt too strange using her sister's name. Did the queen already know the truth and that was why she seemed unsurprised by Meira's question?

"Because the truth is, Your Majesty, that my name is not Eirian," Meira said after a moment. "Eirian was my sister's name. My true name is Meira. I apologize for the deception, but I wanted to make sure I would be able to protect myself before I revealed the truth."

Meira studied the queen's features for a moment, waiting to see if she would be angry. Instead the queen gave her a comforting smile, placing a hand on her shoulder. "I understand completely, my dear. As I've said, you are quite knowledgeable about our ways. I encourage you to keep that knowledge in mind as you journey into the Shadowlands tomorrow, and that you rest and prepare. I will speak with Garvan and Poppy privately and tell them of your true name."

Relief washed over Meira as she realized the queen was not, in fact, angry.

"There is something I'd like for you to know as well, Meira," the queen said. "The maze that you fell into when you first arrived in our lands was not something of my creation. That was something Averith put in place so she could be notified of any humans who make their way into our lands. It was not something I would have chosen to put you through."

Meira nodded. "I appreciate that, Your Majesty. Thank you."

The queen made a gesture with her hand, and Poppy flew over. "Poppy, take Eirian into the tree and help her find a chamber to bathe and sleep in," the queen instructed.

Poppy nodded, and Meira followed her into the tree, relieved at the prospect of slipping into warmer, dry clothes. As she rested in the bed of the guest chamber, she thought of the journey ahead, and the possible dangers lying between her and the tower. Even once she reached Gaelen, what state would she find him in? What if it were too late to save him?

But as her eyes began to drift shut, Meira pushed those doubts to the back of her mind, instead thinking of the

moment she would find Gaelen and what it would be like to
be back in his arms once more.

CHAPTER TEN

Meira rose with the sun the following day, eager to begin the journey to the Shadowlands. After bathing and putting on a short-sleeved green tunic and riding skirt, Meira re-braided her hair to manage it for the journey. Mixed emotions ran through her as she sat for a moment, staring at the pile of supplies. She was excited to *finally* be starting on her quest, but she'd be lying if she said there weren't small doubts in the back of her mind, making her wonder if she'd succeed.

Don't think that way, she thought. *You can do this. You'll find Gaelen and bring him home.*

Meira fiddled with the end of her braid, staring down at the bag of supplies and bedroll. Closing her eyes, she breathed in the fragrance of sweet-smelling flowers nearby. She was finally on her way.

I'm coming, Gaelen.

"Meira, are you ready?"

She looked up to see Garvan standing nearby, his wings tucked in at his sides. Meira nodded, tucking the bedroll under her arm as she stood and grabbing her bag with the other hand. "Yes, I am."

Meira followed the owl to the center of the clearing. As she walked over, her eye caught sight of a beautiful gray horse, already tacked and bridled. She promptly strode over to the horse, carefully approaching and reaching out to scratch the mare's nose. Her heart ached, wishing Vala could have come with her.

"This is Aine," a voice said from behind. "She's quite fond of humans. I thought you two might get along well."

Meira turned to see Lythienne nearby, reaching out to brush the side of Aine's neck. "I do. She reminds me of my horse, Vala. I had to leave her behind to come here."

The queen nodded. "Aine will be a good companion for you, then," she said. "I do have one more thing for you, before you go." A nearby servant stepped forward, carrying a soft pillow with a single obsidian-black arrow on it. "This arrow will be useful, when you have to climb the high walls of Averith's defenses."

Meira picked the arrow up, carefully examining it. "Thank you, Your Majesty."

"The road to the Shadowlands is dangerous. Be cautious as you travel it, and heed Poppy and Garvan. They will advise you faithfully."

"I will. And thank you again for everything you've done for me, Your Majesty," Meira replied, bowing her head.

After placing the arrow carefully inside her quiver, Meira returned to Aine's side, placing her foot up into the stirrup and hoisting herself up onto the saddle. She took the reins, absently rubbing the well-maintained braided leather through her fingertips to test the weight of them before taking her bow sheath and slinging it over her shoulder.

"Hello again, Meira."

Meira looked down as Poppy flew up next to her, her wings fluttering behind her.

"We should get going," Garvan said, coming up on Meira's other side. "We have a long journey ahead of us."

"Good luck, Meira," Queen Lythienne said, stepping back from the horses.

Meira smiled and nodded, clicking her tongue to the roof of her mouth and squeezing the horse's sides, urging her to move forward so their journey could finally begin.

* * *

The afternoon sun pierced through the clouds high above as Meira followed behind Garvan on Aine. They'd been riding for what felt like hours, with a few stops in between to rest, but Meira didn't mind. Her fingers twisted the reins between them as she thought about Gaelen and the journey to the tower he'd been trapped in. What would she find when she finally got there? Would he be hurt, or under some spell, brainwashing him into accepting Averith as his queen? She shuddered, pushing the thoughts out of her mind.

Meira came up next to Garvan as he paused at a hill covered in grass and clovers. The owl waited until Poppy had joined them before raising one of his wings and pointing in the distance.

"Up ahead is the Meligar Woods," Garvan said. "We'll make camp there for the night and let Aine rest."

"How many days will it take to get to the Shadow-lands?" Meira asked.

"That depends on how soon we find its entrance," he said. "The entrance to the shadow queen's lands matches its name—it comes and goes with the shadows, opening the veil between our lands."

"Keep in mind that time passes differently here in the fae lands than it does in the human lands," Poppy added. "A day here could be a week in the human lands."

Meira's eyes widened in realization. When she'd left her father and Haelyn behind, she'd thought she'd be gone for a few days at most. . . but now she may be gone for *months*, without any way to communicate with them and let them know she was alright.

Knowing there was nothing she could do now, Meira nodded, letting out a deep breath. "We should keep going," she said, urging her horse down the hill once more.

They entered the Meligar Woods, making their way to a small clearing. They went about gathering wood for a campfire and setting up for camp. Meira began untacking Aine, removing her saddle, brushing her down, and lastly giving her food and water before tying her lead rope to a tree.

Meira stared at the flames from her bedroll, her legs tucked up to her chest with her arms wrapped around them. Garvan sat perched on a branch above the camp, and Poppy sat opposite Meira.

"What can you tell me about Queen Averith? How would she have been able to trick the court into believing she was human?" Meira asked.

"Probably with some kind of a glamour," Garvan answered, a pipe held tight in his beak.

"What's glamour?" Meira asked.

"It's a spell to change your appearance," he said. "It wouldn't have been hard for her to use it to look human and trick the king and members of the court, especially if they're among those who are, ah, non-believers in our kind."

Meira nodded. "What can we expect from her once we reach the Shadowlands?"

"She has creatures to do her bidding," Poppy said. "Whatever you do, don't let them touch you, or you'll turn into a shadow just like them."

"There are three different kinds of shadow creatures," Garvan said. "There are the Shadowlings, who can change their form to look like someone else, the Specters, who manipulate shadows, and the Shades. It is only the last sort who can turn others into shadows with a simple touch."

Meira shuddered at the thought. She took a deep breath, glancing up at the open canopy where she could see the stars twinkling above.

"Meira, how did you come to know so much about our ways?" Poppy asked.

Meira smiled fondly. "My father," she answered. "I would sit by the fireplace when I was a child, listening as he told me stories of ancient beings roaming the earth."

"He sounds like a wise man," Garvan said. "There was a time, many years ago, when we roamed among humans more openly. As time went on, we found that humans were less accepting of our ways, so we faded away, returning to our homeland."

Meira nodded, shifting around on her bedroll.

"You should get some sleep," Poppy said. "We'll keep watch over the camp. The shadows are at their strongest when there is less light to impact them, so we will need to rise with the sun and keep going."

Too exhausted to argue, Meira nodded, stifling a yawn. Her body still ached from her fight with the mud monster, and she knew they still had a long journey ahead of them.

She lay back on her bedroll, watching the flames until finally her eyes became too heavy and she drifted off to sleep.

* * *

Meira climbed through the window of the dark tower. A candle flickered to life, and she looked over at the bed up against the wall. Gaelen sat there with a book sprawled open on his lap, a grin on his face. She returned his smile, walking over and bending down to plant a soft kiss on his lips, no words passing between them.

A dark cloud passed over them as the scene changed. She was still in the tower, but this time Gaelen stood in front of her, a pained look on his face. She called out for him, stretching her arms out as far as she could, but could not touch him.

* * *

Meira woke with a gasp, bolting up from the bedroll, trying to clasp on to her surroundings and steady her breathing. The campfire had died down some time during the night, leaving only a few smoking embers, barely showing any flame. Garvan lay on a tree branch above, leaning against the trunk with his eyes closed and wings resting on his feathered chest, while Poppy lay on the ground across from Meira.

It was only a dream.

CHAPTER ELEVEN

A few days had passed since they set out to the Shadowlands, and they had yet to find the entrance. Meira couldn't help her frustration. Surely they should have found it by now! But she trusted her companions and knew they wouldn't lead her astray. The path they'd followed so far ultimately meant finding Gaelen, even if it wasn't on the timetable she'd hoped for. Finding him at all would be enough.

They stopped at a stream to rest. Meira led Aine to the edge of the river, dropping her reins. She knelt a few feet away, scooping her palms into the water and lifting it to her face, letting it wash over her. She was dirty and tired, but they still had a long way to go.

Aine snorted nearby, and Meira glanced up to see the horse bobbing her head up and down—a sign of nervousness. A shiver ran up her spine as Meira looked around. A twig snapped, and she stood up slowly, turning toward the source, but found nothing.

Maybe I'm more tired than I thought.

Aine snorted again as Meira finished washing her hands

in the stream and went to Aine's side, gently stroking the horse's muzzle. "Easy, girl," she murmured.

Meira turned away from the horse just as two black figures entered the area. At first, Meira thought they were just wearing black cloaks, but when she looked closer, she saw the underbrush through their approaching forms.

Shadows.

Meira's mouth gaped open in shock, uncertain of what to do. Should she scream? Run? Keeping her eyes on the shadows, she took a slow step back.

Poppy and Garvan ran toward her at full tilt, with more shadows on their heels. "Go, Meira!" Poppy yelled.

One of the shadows came up behind Poppy, grabbing at her arms. The shadow's long fingers curled around her arm, yanking her back. Poppy's body lay suspended in midair, her lips parted in shock as her body slowly faded into nothing.

"Poppy, no!" Meira's eyes widened in horror.

"Go, Meira! Don't worry about us," Garvan yelled, landing next to her.

Meira shook her head. "I can't leave you here!"

Shadows popped up around them like daisies from a late frost, some appearing behind trees and others behind rocks. She reached over her shoulder for her bow, grabbing an arrow out of the quill. Turning, Meira sucked in a breath and nocked an arrow, sighting along its length to line up her target before letting it fly. The shadow merely hovered in place, completely unfazed by the arrow that had just gone through it.

Garvan touched her arm with his wing. "Meira, the arrows won't work on them. Just go while you still can," he said.

Meira wanted to protest again, but the evidence in front

of her eyes had proven them right. She had to keep going. She turned and ran back to where she'd left Aine by the stream and hoisted herself onto the horse's back. Pulling on the reins, she turned Aine to face the stream. Water splashed up at her as Aine rode across it. Garvan's scream echoed in the air behind her as they reached the other side. Meira looked across the water as a shadow touched its long black fingers to Garvan's arm.

"No!" Meira yanked on Aine's reins, turning the horse back toward the riverbank. She gritted her teeth, fighting the urge to go back.

I'm so sorry, Garvan, she thought, helplessly watching from across the way. What would happen to Gaelen if she stayed and tried to help Garvan? Shaking her head, she spurred the horse into running again, leaving the stream behind.

Meira looked behind her and realized the shadows no longer followed her. She gently tugged on the reins, and Aine slowed to a walk in response, allowing Meira to search for a place to rest. Finally, she found a rock ledge that seemed safe enough to hide under. She climbed off of Aine's back and tied the reins to a nearby tree, crouching beneath the ledge.

Tucking her legs to her chest, Meira wrapped her arms around them, doing her level best to ignore her chattering teeth as the bitter wind moved against her. She thought of Poppy and Garvan and couldn't help but feel guilty for leaving them behind. Letting out a shuddering breath, she forced herself to close her eyes. Exhaustion soon pulled her into a dreamless sleep.

* * *

Meira woke early the next morning as the bright sun gleamed against the rock ledge, shining into her eyes. She opened her eyes slowly, trying to recollect her thoughts and remember where she was. Aine stood nearby, nibbling at the leaves within reach of her tie. The memories filtered back with a pang of regret as she remembered what had happened to Garvan and Poppy.

Meira stood from beneath the ledge, careful not to bump her head on it, and walked to Aine's side, brushing her hand along the mare's neck.

"Well, now what do we do, Aine?" she mused, looking around. Her stomach grumbled from hunger, and she searched the woods for any sign of berries that she could eat, hungry enough to take the chance by eating fae food.

Walking a few feet away, Meira knelt near a bush with purple berries on it. Cautiously, she pulled a few into her palm, carefully examining them. Aine bobbed her head up and down, and for a split second, Meira thought she saw the horse's eyes change and show an image of Queen Lythienne. Meira blinked, shaking her head. Surely it had to be a trick of the light, or perhaps just pure exhaustion. Still. . . was it possible that Queen Lythienne had given Aine to her for a reason—that it was her way of keeping an eye on Meira during her journey?

Meira turned back to the berries, remembering what Queen Lythienne had said when she'd previously offered her food and said that it would extend beyond her territory.

"Here it goes," Meira said, popping a berry into her mouth. The juice flowed onto her tongue, and her stomach grumbled again as she swallowed. After a few moments, nothing happened, and she sighed in relief that they seemed to be safe. She pulled a pouch from her waist and filled it with berries.

After collecting as many as she could, Meira walked to Aine's side and pulled herself up onto the horse's back. "Come on, Aine. We've still got a long way to go," she said.

Meira rode Aine in the direction they'd been heading until she'd stopped under the ledge for the night, hoping it was the right way. As they rode, the wind shifted, bringing on a cool breeze. She shuddered, pulling her cloak closer and glancing up at the sky, where a large dark cloud blocked the afternoon sun.

Aine bopped her head up and down and slowed as they approached the entrance to a long bridge. Meira dismounted and pulled the horse's reins toward the entrance. Wind whipped at her cloak and braid as she stepped closer to the bridge, sending chills down her spine.

A swirl of green wind moved across the grass and stopped in front of the bridge, sending Meira flying back. She fell hard to the ground on her back, knocking the air out of her. Behind her, Aine reared up on her hind legs.

Meira looked up from where she lay on the ground, using her elbows to hold her up. The green wind swirl faded away. In its place stood Averith, towering over the bridge's entrance, her appearance changed in several striking ways. Pointed ears stuck out beneath long black curls of hair. Her eyes were larger than that of a normal human, black and shiny, and she had long black fingernails.

Meira pushed herself off the ground, staring at the woman towering in front of her. Aine came up behind Meira, and she grabbed at the horse's reins, reaching a comforting hand up to rub the horse's nose.

"Lady Meira," the queen sneered. "I have to say, I wouldn't have expected you to come this far."

Meira raised her chin defiantly. "You'd be surprised what I am capable of. Where is Prince Gaelen?"

The queen smirked. "I have come to offer you a deal, Lady Meira—one you'd be smart to take me up on. Gaelen is lost to you now, and his kingdom is mine. Turn back while you still have the chance, and you can return home."

Meira shook her head, clutching the reins tight in her hand. "Never. I *will* find Gaelen, and we will stop you from taking over his kingdom once and for all."

"Are you sure about that, Meira?" the queen asked. "Perhaps I can sweeten the deal."

Meira kept her chin raised, choosing to stay silent. Whatever deal the queen thought she could offer Meira, she would never agree to it.

"What if I could bring your sister back to life? You'd like that, wouldn't you—for her to be alive, and healthy, and for your family to be together again?" she continued. "I will bring your sister back, if you agree to turn back now and leave Gaelen and his kingdom to me. And just to make the deal even sweeter, I will make your father healthy again as well."

Meira stared at the queen. Clearly, as a fae, the queen was powerful—powerful enough to remove all the servants from the castle and trap Gaelen in the Shadowlands. Would she be powerful enough to bring Eirian back from the dead *and* heal her father as well? An image of her together with her sister and father once more came to her mind. Her heart felt heavy. She wanted it, more than anything...

But not at the cost of Gaelen.

Her sister was gone. But Gaelen... Gaelen was still here, almost within reach.

Meira shook her head. "No. I won't make any deals with you. I *will* find and save Gaelen and his kingdom."

The queen laughed, tossing her head back. "You think

you can stop *me*? We'll just see about that. I'll be seeing you again soon enough, Lady Meira."

Green swirls appeared at the bottom of the queen's legs, wrapping around them and moving upwards, covering her whole body and disappearing her from sight.

Meira let out a breath, turning and placing a hand on the side of Aine's neck, trying to process what she'd just seen. Thoughts of doubt crept into the back of her mind. *I'm no match for Averith. What if I can't defeat her?*

Shaking her head, Meira pushed the thoughts away and started walking toward the bridge again, taking careful steps. Stepping onto the edge of the bridge, she stared out into the distance, feeling her stomach drop. It went out as far as she could see, with no handrails, over a seemingly bottomless ravine. Meira's eyes widened, suddenly very aware of just how high up the bridge was.

I can't do this, she thought, her breathing heavy as she turned away. She leaned up against Aine's side, resting her arms over the saddle as she fought to steady her breathing.

Heights didn't bother Meira—normally. Even the stairs she'd climbed in the maze hadn't bothered her. But this bridge was far worse than the stairs, or anything else she'd ever climbed. What if she fell? What if the bridge had no end and she was stuck high above a gorge with nothing to hold on to?

Gaelen, she thought, closing her eyes. She remembered the dream she'd had the night before of him disappearing and knew she had to keep going. Taking a deep breath, Meira made sure her pack, quiver, and bow were secure on her back. She then moved to stand in front of Aine, reaching up to scratch the mare on her nose.

"This is as far as you can go, Aine," she said. "Thank you for bringing me as far as you have. You can go home now."

The mare bumped the end of her soft muzzle against Meira's face. Meira smiled in spite of herself and watched as the mare turned away, cantering off into the distance.

Once Aine was gone, Meira turned back to the bridge and approached its edge. That there was nothing to hold on to while crossing terrified her, but it had to be done, regardless of the pit of dread that formed in her stomach. Keeping her head held high, gaze fixed straight ahead, Meira took a step onto the bridge, holding her arms out from her sides. She raised each foot carefully, one after the other. She couldn't go back, which meant the only way was forward. Meira intended to go as far as she needed to, to do whatever she needed to do.

Wind tugged and pushed at Meira as she carefully crossed the bridge, doing her best to concentrate on her footing and not think about anything else—or that if she took one misstep, she could fall to her doom.

Meira. . . Meira. . .

Meira turned as the voice called out to her, suddenly forgetting that the bridge was thin and didn't give much room for movement. Her arms flailed as she lost her balance, her boot slipping on the wood. Meira screamed, grabbing hold to the side of the bridge with one hand, her legs flailing beneath her.

Grabbing on to the wood with her other hand, she used all the strength in her arms to carefully pull herself back up onto the bridge, hugging the thin wood with her arms beneath it as she tried to catch her breath. Tears streamed down her cheeks, both from the harsh wind and relief that she'd been able to catch herself.

Once she'd caught her breath, Meira looked straight ahead, staring out at the end of the bridge, which was finally in sight, maybe ten feet away. Pulling herself carefully up onto her knees, and then on her feet, she kept walking, hastening her pace.

Meira reached the end of the bridge. A wave of relief washed over her when she stepped onto solid ground. Once she'd slowed her breathing, she looked over her shoulder. That voice she'd heard. . . her heart filled with sadness, remembering a time that no longer was.

After a while of walking, Meira reached the edge of the forest. There, in the distance, she saw a land of endless rocks and dirt, with gray clouds hovering above. The cool breeze tugged fitfully at her cloak as she stared at the same tall vine-cloaked tower she'd seen in her dreams, and she knew she'd found Gaelen's prison.

Adrenaline ran through Meira as she hastened her stride. Her body begged her to stop and rest, but she knew she couldn't. *I'm too close now.* After walking along a long dirt path, she stopped at the edge of it as she came face to face with a pair of tall iron gates, with vines tangled through their bars. High above, the clouds were dark and gray.

Meira carefully made her way through the gates, looking around for any sign of the queen or her shadow creatures, and entered a garden. Some parts of the garden had high walls covered in a carpet of moss and vines, while others had bushes of withered flowers. She followed the path, turning down one row after another. While she walked the gardens, Meira's mind flashed back to the maze she'd been thrown into upon entering the fae lands, and she wondered if she'd be met with more of the same traps.

Meira turned through a brick archway leading into the center of the garden, where she was met with the wide base of a tower. The tangle of thorns that clung to its sides were so thick she couldn't see the stonework beneath, with an even thicker carpet of mossy vines looming over her head on either side of the tall walls surrounding the tower. She searched the bottom tier for any sign of an entrance, but she saw none. How did the queen trap Gaelen in the tower if there was no entrance?

"Gaelen?" she called.

Silence.

Meira looked around the garden, listening for any sign of more shadow creatures, not knowing if Averith had them keeping guard. After a moment, a shadow appeared above her, and she glanced up to see Gaelen looking down at her from the window.

"Meira? What are you doing here?" he asked.

"There's no time to explain. Can you throw me something to climb up the wall?"

"Just a moment," Gaelen called, stepping away. He soon returned and leaned out the window and began to lower something toward her. It was long and thin, like a rope, but it moved oddly.

As the rope neared, Meira reached out to grasp it. Instead of grabbing on to the rope though, her hand went through it, as though it were transparent. Meira frowned, reaching out again to grasp it, but the same thing happened.

"I can't seem to grab it," Meira called up to him. "Do you have anything else I can use?"

Gaelen shook his head. "We need to hurry, before the queen comes."

Meira chewed on the inside of her lip, trying to think of what else she could use to climb the wall, before she remembered the arrow Queen Lythienne had given her. "I have an idea. Move away from the window."

Once Gaelen was out of sight, Meira pulled her bow off

her back and placed it on the ground then removed her pack. She reached into her bag and pulled a rope out. She then reached into her quiver and pulled out the enchanted arrow Lythienne had given her, tying the rope around the end of it.

Meira nocked the arrow, her fingers curling into place. Taking a deep breath, she drew the string back and held it for a few seconds before letting the arrow fly into the tower window. She waited a moment before beginning the climb up the wall, careful of the thorny vines surrounding its bottom.

I'm coming, Gaelen.

CHAPTER TWELVE

Meira used all her strength to pull herself along the rope. Her arms and shoulders burned from the effort of it all, while her booted feet carefully trod up the brick tower as she climbed higher and higher. Walking up along the wall felt strange, almost dizzying due to the orientation of the horizon, and what she could touch were at such odds with one another. After finally reaching the top, she grabbed on to the edge of the windowsill, pulling herself up over the edge.

Meira leaned back against the wall as she caught her breath, not daring to look behind her and out the window. Instead, she peered into the darkened room she'd just entered. She yanked on the rope and pulled it and the arrow down, untying the arrow from the rope and sticking it back into her quiver. She wrapped the rope up and put it back into her bag as she looked around the room.

"Gaelen?"

Candlelight sprang to life in the corner, its shadows bouncing against the walls. Gaelen appeared from the shadows wearing the same tunic he'd worn the last time she saw him. Meira caught her breath as they made eye contact for the first time in weeks, and he walked toward her. She stared at him for a moment, wondering if it were truly him or if one of the fae's cruel illusions was playing with her mind again. But as he closed the distance, she saw something in his eyes that the illusion hadn't had: love.

It's him. It's really him.

Visibly concerned, Gaelen asked, "Meira, what are you doing here?"

"I came to find you," she said. "I've missed you, Gaelen. I'm so happy you're alright. I didn't know what had happened to you…"

Gaelen rushed forward, placing a hand on Meira's arm as he lowered his head and pressed a hard kiss to her lips. Meira inhaled his scent as they savored one another, a mix of emotions washing over her. Reluctantly breaking the kiss, she leaned her head against him as she felt his rushing heartbeat and closed her eyes.

I'd forgotten how much I missed this, she thought. For a moment, she forgot where they were. It felt as though she were back home and this was all but a dream.

"Gaelen, she's coming. I saw her at the bridge, and she tried to offer me a deal. I have to get you out of here," Meira said, looking up at him. Gaelen stepped back, turning his head away from her. Frowning, Meira placed a hand on one of his arms. "What's wrong?"

Sadness filled his eyes even as his smile faded. "You shouldn't have come."

Meira shook her head. "What do you mean I shouldn't have come? Of course I should have."

Fear crept into her chest. Had the illusion she met in the

maze been right? Had Gaelen chosen to stay in the Shadow-lands after all?

Gaelen turned his back to her. "I can't leave."

"I don't understand. What's happened to you?" she asked.

Gaelen sighed and turned back to her. He took her hand, leading her over to the window. "Watch," he said. He stretched his arm out the window, leaving it there. After a few seconds, his arm changed, turning black, and then almost fading. He gritted his teeth, standing at an angle that didn't obstruct her view. She almost wished it did.

Meira gasped. "What is *that?*"

Gaelen pulled his arm back in. "A shadow," he said, a pained look on his face as his arm reappeared.

Meira reached out for his arm, pulling it close to her so she could look it over. *Just like in my dream*, she thought, horrified. "Oh, Gaelen. . . what did she do to you?" she whispered, fighting to hold back her tears.

"A curse," Gaelen said. "If I leave the tower, I turn into a shadow. I'll disappear and lose myself forever."

Meira took a shuddering breath. "Is there a way to break the curse?"

"I don't know," Gaelen murmured.

"Why has she done all of this? If she wanted your crown, why wouldn't she have just taken it?" Meira asked.

"Because if she can magically share the kingdom with me through marriage, she can have control over both the fairy and human lands," he said, pulling her with him to settle on the bed. "That's why she's trapped me here. As long as I'm out of the way and unable to marry, she can wait and take the crown. But if I marry before then, she no longer has a claim to it."

Meira watched Gaelen with wide eyes, uncertain of

what to say. The time she'd spent with him had been such a whirlwind before his disappearance. She thought back to the conversation she'd had with her father. She still wanted to marry Gaelen, more than anything, and she would fight to make it happen. That meant stopping the queen once and for all.

Meira stood from the bed, walking toward the window. "How *does* the queen get up here, anyway?"

"With my own shadow," Gaelen said, standing and following behind her. "She forces me to drop it down to her like a rope so she can climb it, just to cause me more suffering."

Meira frowned. How could the queen have used his shadow to climb the wall? Her eyes widened in horror after a moment, suddenly realizing. "Is that why you weren't able to help me climb up the wall? Because it was your shadow?"

Gaelen nodded. "She takes her time climbing it every time, so that I have to keep it there just a little longer," he said. "She comes here every day, asking if I've changed my mind yet about sharing the kingdom with her, expecting me to break."

Meira tried her best to hide her grimace, taking a shuddering breath as she looked up at him.

He smiled, reaching out to cup her cheek. "It would have been worth it, had it worked for you, though." Leaning in, Gaelen planted a soft kiss on her lips.

Meira closed her eyes, wishing this were all just some horrible nightmare. "I'm sorry, Gaelen," she said after a moment, breaking the kiss. "You don't deserve any of this."

Gaelen shook his head. "This isn't your fault, Meira," he said.

"She can't get away with this. There has to be something we can do to stop her, once and for all. We have to stop the curse, which means we have to stop the queen."

"How, though? She's powerful, and she has the advantage of being in her homeland."

Meira reached into the pouch on her belt and carefully pulled out the sun stone, holding it out for Gaelen to see. "With this."

"What is it?" Gaelen asked.

"It's called Amiroth's Sun Stone," she answered. "I used it against a mud monster, the stone's guardian. The queen of the Woodland fairies said I would need this gemstone in the Shadowlands, and I think this is why."

"It's too dangerous, Meira," Gaelen said, shaking his head. "If the queen sees you up here, I don't know what she'll do. You should just forget about me and go."

Meira shook her head, stepping away from Gaelen. "No," she said firmly, her voice angry as another hot tear rolled down her cheek. "I won't leave you here, not after everything I've gone through to find you. I've been trapped in mazes and walls, I've been pricked by thorns that made me hallucinate, I was chased by a mud monster through a swamp. I lost two friends to Averith's shadows. I've come too far after all that to just allow you to give up. Your people need you. *I* need you."

The queen could come at any moment, and then what? I don't care, she thought. Throwing caution to the wind, she rushed toward him, grabbing the front of his tunic to yank his head down so she could kiss him, her heart pounding. After a moment, she pulled back, looking up at him.

"I love you, Gaelen. Don't leave me," she whispered.

Gaelen's gaze sharpened. "Oh, Meira," he whispered back, leaning his forehead down against hers. "I won't leave you, ever. I . . ."

"Gaelen!"

Meira froze, staring at Gaelen as she realized whose voice called.

The queen was outside the tower, and Meira was inside, with no door to escape through. Meira looked frantically around Gaelen's room, eyes wide.

"It's the queen," Gaelen said softly, lifting his head. "She can't see you here."

"What do we do?" she whispered.

Gaelen took her hand, leading her over to the wooden wardrobe tucked in the corner of the tower. He opened the door, glancing inside to make sure there was enough room. "Hide in here. No matter what you hear, don't come out, and don't make a sound until I tell you it's safe," he said.

"*Gaelen!* I don't like to be kept waiting," the queen's voice called.

"Hurry," Gaelen whispered.

Meira stepped into the wardrobe, taking her bow off her back and placing it by her boots inside. She stood with her back straight against the wall as far back as she could. Once she was in position, she nodded, and Gaelen closed the door, leaving her with only a sliver of light peeking through the crack.

Meira watched from the wardrobe as Gaelen straightened his collar then walked over to the window. He bent down over the windowsill, and after a few minutes, the queen appeared outside the window, pulling her legs over the windowsill and stepping into the room. She walked into the center, her long dark dress gliding across the floor. Behind her, two shadow creatures with bright white eyes appeared and moved farther into the tower.

"What kept you?" the queen asked, her tone dark.

"I apologize, Stepmother. I fell asleep reading my book and did not hear your call," Gaelen said.

"I see," the queen replied.

Meira shuddered at the queen's tone. Did the queen suspect something was wrong?

After an expectant pause, the queen said, "I take it you still have not reconsidered my offer."

Gaelen walked away from the window, turning his back to the queen. "I've given you my answer. Do as you will to me, but you will never have my crown."

Gaelen faced his stepmother, about to say something more, when thick shadowy vines shot down from above and wrapped themselves around his arms, pulling them away from his sides. Below, vines snaked their way up his legs and chest. Sharp thorns grew out of the vines, pulling tight on him as blood dribbled down his skin. Gaelen screamed, thrashing.

The queen walked toward him slowly, reaching up to grab a chunk of Gaelen's hair, yanking his head downward. "I grow tired of your stubbornness, Gaelen," she said. "I will break you, one way or another. If my little curse isn't enough, perhaps finding that little maid you were courting will."

Meira shifted within the wardrobe at the queen's words, wishing she could lash out at Averith for her daring. Her fingers curled into fists as she steadied her breathing while she watched the queen and Gaelen.

Gaelen yanked his head up, pulling his hair out of the queen's grasp, and glared at her. "You leave her alone," he growled.

The queen gave a wicked smile, turning away from Gaelen. Meira eased the doors open and carefully slid out of the wardrobe, tiptoeing toward Gaelen. Averith's eyes flashed toward the mirror in the corner, attracted by the movement, and Meira found herself staring into the queen's reflected eyes.

"You! What are you doing here?" the queen growled, turning toward the shadow creatures. "Get her!"

"No! Meira!" Gaelen yelled, pulling at the vines. "Get away from her!"

"You just couldn't leave well enough alone, could you?" snarled Averith, her eyes glinting with malice. "I tire of your meddling. Gaelen can watch my pets rip you apart, limb from limb—it'll be the last thing he ever sees."

The shadows descended on Meira like a pack of wild dogs, ferocious and relentless, their ghostly forms swirling and snarling. The weight of their bodies smashed against her, muffling her cries as she tumbled to the ground, their rough, clawed hands leaving scratches and cuts on her skin. Meira threw up her hands to shield her face from the assault, her body contorted and twisted in a desperate attempt to escape. Amidst the chaos, she saw Gaelen, his jaw clenched, his muscles straight as he fought against the vines.

Meira kicked at the shadows, but her kicks phased through them. They pressed down on her, their low, guttural growls blowing frigid breath against her face and causing her skin to crawl. Holding them off with one arm, her free hand fumbled for the sun stone nestled in the pouch on her belt. Her fingertips had brushed against the soft material when the queen turned to Gaelen.

Tendrils of green magic flitted from the queen's fingers toward Gaelen. The tendrils took on a life of their own, snaking around Gaelen's legs and up his body. The vines that bound him grew lax as the magic progressed until it was just below his chin. He cried out in pain as he was lifted into the air, levitating dangerously close to the window.

"Gaelen, no!" Meira called out. She thrashed against the shadows, but their grips were strong. Her heart thudded against her chest. Gaelen's words screamed in her mind: *If I leave the tower, I'll turn into a shadow. I'll disappear and lose myself forever.* She opened her mouth to scream, but no words came out.

Her eyes widened in horror as the air outside the window touched Gaelen. He froze. His face contorted, melting away into darkness. Everything that had once been Gaelen stripped away in a matter of seconds, with only a shadow left in its wake.

Averith threw her head back and laughed. She released Gaelen from his restraints as he floated to her side. "What do you think of your precious prince now?"

The shadows holding onto Meira released her and allowed her to scramble to her feet. Sweat dripped from her forehead, her breathing heavy as she took a few tentative steps forward.

"Gaelen?"

Gaelen's body was black with the same hooked claw shape to his hands as the shadows. His mouth was a thin white line and his eyes two large white holes. Not really eyes at all. They stared back at her without a hint of emotion. A lump rose in Meira's throat.

This wasn't the man she knew.

Gaelen was gone.

"Poor Meira," the queen said, lips curling upward. "What will you do now that your beloved prince is gone? And to think his last sight was my pets clawing at you. Gaelen's kingdom is mine now. I almost pity you, except. . . I can't have witnesses."

Gaelen lunged toward Meira, his fingers outstretched as if to strangle her. She darted away, but he caught hold of her braid, yanking it so hard that her head snapped back. Her vision went white. He snatched the back of her tunic and slammed her into the ground. The taste of blood filled her mouth as she bit down on her lip from the impact. Meira wheezed. Before she could react, Gaelen was on top of her. His blackened hands closed around her throat.

"Gaelen, please. I don't want to fight you," Meira pleaded, pulling at his hands. That only made his grip tighten.

The pressure on her throat was unrelenting, crushing her windpipe and cutting off her air supply. Her lungs burned, desperate for oxygen that seemed just out of reach. Meira looked into the face of who was once her beloved. Her heart ached, and tears burned hot at the corners of her eyes.

I failed, she thought. Her grip loosened. *I couldn't save Poppy, or Garvan. I couldn't save Gaelen. . .*

Giving up was easier. As the room spun around her and dark spots danced at the edges of her vision, the world started slipping away. Meira's hands fell to her sides. A feeling of warmth swelled within her—a peace that beckoned her to close her eyes and fall asleep. She wanted it to envelop her like a blanket and take her to her mother. To her sister.

Meira. . . Meira. . .

A voice whispered into her ringing ears. Meira glanced past Gaelen's shoulder, and her eyes widened at the face smiling down at her—Eirian, healthy, and as she'd always remembered her. Meira's lips parted as she tried to call out her name.

It's not your time, Meira. Don't give up.

Eirian's smile broadened as she faded away. In that moment of suffocating darkness, a surge of adrenaline coursed through Meira's veins.

I'm not giving up.

She once more reached for the sun stone in her pouch. Her hand tingled with numbness, but she shoved it into the pouch and grabbed the sun stone. Its warmth radiated throughout her body. *I'm sorry, Gaelen.*

Ignoring the searing pain in her side and the pulsing ache in her head, Meira tugged out the sunstone and pushed it toward his face. Its bright glow caused Gaelen to let out a sickening screech as he released his hold and rolled away from her, holding his eyes as they sizzled smoke.

Gasping and choking, Meira rolled onto her side and touched her throat. The world around her sharpened with each rattled breath. She pushed herself to her feet, lifting her chin high as she faced the queen.

"Amiroth's stone," Averith hissed. She narrowed her eyes, waving her shadows to her as she stepped back.

Standing together, all the shadows looked the same.

Which one was Gaelen?

Meira's grip on the stone tightened. She could destroy the queen and her shadows once and for all, but how would she do so without killing Gaelen? Quiet tears rolled down her cheeks as she began to shiver. Gaelen wouldn't want his kingdom to fall into the fae queen's hands. Even if it meant giving up his life to stop her.

"Gaelen's kingdom will never be yours," she spat. "I'll never allow it."

Taking one last look at the shadows, Meira raised the stone toward the queen, unveiling its blinding light. Meira closed her eyes and looked away, feeling the raw power unleash from the stone. It pulsated in her head until she felt an explosion of power burst from it. The last thing she heard was the shadows screeching and the queen's screams.

Meira dropped to her knees, the stone rolling from her hand, its light fading as she held herself in her arms. Once the light had fully faded, she opened her eyes to find herself alone. Everyone was gone—including Gaelen.

CHAPTER THIRTEEN

Seeing no sign of Gaelen, panic filled Meira's chest. She got up and ran to the window, looking below, where she saw a black spot covering the ground.

"Gaelen!" she yelled frantically.

Silence.

Meira blinked back her tears aggressively before shaking her head, trying to wrap her mind around what had happened. Everything had happened so fast—the light from the sun stone had been so bright, she'd barely been able to see the queen and shadows fall out the window.

I killed Gaelen.

Meira fell hard to her knees, the tears she fought to hold back now opened like a broken dam, covering her face with her hands.

"Meira," a distant voice called.

It sounded like him, but. . . *I must be hearing things*, she told herself.

"Meira!" the voice called again, this time closer.

Lowering her hands from her face, Meira looked up. She sniffed, slowly standing up and approaching the window.

The sky had shifted to a bright blue, the moody clouds fading away as the sunlight filtered through their remains. The landscape, which had been dark and gray mere moments ago, was now lush and green, with wild and plant life blooming all around. Servants Meira recognized from the castle filtered into the garden, looking around with confused gazes, some covering their eyes as they adjusted to the light. Her eyes widened in realization. The servants must have been turned to shadows by the queen, and now they were free.

Using the rope and arrow she'd used to climb the tower, Meira rappelled down. When she reached the bottom, she turned around.

There, standing several feet in front of her, was Gaelen, alive. He turned his arms, studying them closely as he stepped out farther into the sunlight, as though to make sure it wasn't some trick. He spread his hands out before him, looking them over.

"Gaelen," Meira whispered. "Is it really you?"

Gaelen looked up at her, flashing his familiar grin. "Yes, Meira. It's me."

As Meira rushed toward him, Gaelen laughed, picking her up by the waist and spinning her around in the air. He set her down after a moment, and Meira wrapped her arms tightly around him.

"Ow," Gaelen said after a moment.

Meira pulled back, looking down at his arms as he turned them over. Long scratches from the vines lined his arms, with trails of dried blood snaking down them.

"Gaelen, you're hurt," Meira said, taking one of his arms into her hands. She reached behind her and grabbed the bottom of her cloak, tearing a long strip of fabric from its bottom. She carefully wrapped it around his arm, tying it off once she ran out of fabric.

"Gaelen, I... I thought I'd never see you again. I thought I'd lost you," Meira said after she finished tying it.

Gaelen smiled, reaching up to caress her cheek as he shook his head. "You didn't lose me, Meira. I will always be here for you."

Meira returned his smile as Gaelen tipped her chin up. She sucked in a breath, looking up into his eyes as she placed a hand on his arm. He leaned in to meet her.

* * *

Meira and Gaelen walked hand in hand through the tower's gardens, searching for others now released from their shadowy prison. They gathered them at the tower, a menagerie of humans and fairies alike. Together for the first time in centuries. Meira's heart swelled at the sight.

Squeezing Gaelen's hand, she guided the group out of the gardens toward the bridge where Meira had crossed into the Shadowlands. Meira was relieved to see it had been replaced by a wider bridge with handrails—how, she didn't know. Perhaps Averith's magic had faded away with her death, removing her spells along with it.

Meira stopped at the edge of the bridge, her mouth gaped open in surprise. Aine waited for them up ahead, grazing on some grass. "Aine?" she asked.

Meira and Gaelen stepped off the bridge as they approached the mare, who whinnied in greeting.

"Is she a friend of yours?" Gaelen asked.

Meira nodded. "Queen Lythienne of the Woodland Court let me borrow her so I could come find you. When I got to the bridge, I had to leave her behind."

Gaelen reached a hand up to pet the side of Aine's neck. "Maybe she's here to bring us home."

* * *

Fairies of all sizes waved and cheered as Meira and Gaelen paraded through Queen Lythienne's court. Musicians blared celebratory music, and sprites danced above them, leaving behind trails of magic. From her throne, Queen Lythienne smiled at the couple as they dismounted from Aine. "Congratulations, Meira," Queen Lythienne said as Meira and Gaelen approached the throne. "I knew you'd be able to do it."

Meira bowed her head. "Thank you, Your Majesty. I couldn't have done it without Poppy and Garvan's help. I'm just sorry I wasn't able to save them from the shadows."

"I wouldn't say that, Meira."

Meira turned to see both Garvan and Poppy standing there, unharmed. Garvan's wide yellow eyes beamed at her as he shuffled his wings. Poppy stood next to him, her purple wings fluttering behind her, grinning broadly at Meira.

"Poppy! Garvan!"

Laughing, Meira stepped away from Gaelen and pulled the owl and fairy into a group hug. Poppy laughed, while Garvan awkwardly hugged his wings around Meira, chuckling.

Meira let go of the owl and fairy, stepping back to Gaelen's side and turning to Queen Lythienne. "Your Majesty, may I present Prince Gaelen Kyrell of the Alythian Kingdom."

Gaelen stepped forward, bowing to the queen. "Your Majesty. It is an honor to meet you."

Queen Lythienne bowed her head in return, smiling. "The honor is mine, Prince Gaelen. You have a very brave betrothed," the queen said.

Meira felt the heat rise to her cheeks. "Ah, well. . . we're not actually engaged, Your Majesty."

Queen Lythienne laughed and nodded. "Well, then, perhaps you should be."

Meira thought back to her seemingly distant conversation with Gaelen about marriage in the forest. She looked up at him as he gave her hand a gentle squeeze, as though letting her know that he, too, was thinking of that conversation.

"In the meantime, however, I have a proposal of my own for you, Prince Gaelen. You may not be aware of this, but many years ago, both fairy and humankind lived amongst each other in peace. I would like to propose an alliance between our two kingdoms, to become official once you are crowned king," Queen Lythienne said. She reached a hand out toward Gaelen.

Gaelen bowed his head. "I would be honored, Your Majesty." He stepped forward, placing a hand in Lythienne's and shaking it.

After Gaelen and Lythienne shook hands, the queen then turned to Meira. "Come here, child."

Meira let go of Gaelen's hand, stepping forward and moving to the queen's side.

"Meira, your sacrifices will never be forgotten," the queen began. "Your courage and determination in rescuing Prince Gaelen have resulted in not only his salvation but the restoration of many lost fairies and humans as well."

The queen gestured with her hand, and a servant approached, carrying a soft pillow. The queen reached toward the pillow and picked up a silver chain with a single white pearl hanging from it, holding her hand out. Meira gasped, her eyes widening as she immediately recognized the precious pearl belonging to her mother. Tears threatened her eyes as she stared at it, hardly believing what was happening.

"I name you Meira the Cursebreaker, Ambassador and Friend of the Fae," the queen continued.

Lythienne unclasped the necklace and placed the chain around Meira's neck, letting it fall to her chest once it was clasped. Meira looked up at the queen with happy tears running down her cheeks.

EPILOGUE

The castle grounds bustled with excitement as the staff rushed around preparing for Prince Gaelen's ceremony to be crowned king, following his twenty-first birthday. Gaelen and the Ivory Council had been working together for the last year to fix the mess Averith had left in her wake. Townspeople chatted to each other with excitement at the prospect of a new king—one who would be a good, kind ruler and follow in his father's footsteps.

When Meira and Gaelen had reached Alythia, Meira had found her father and cousin. She'd never forget the tears of happiness and relief in her father's blue eyes as he warmly pulled her into a hug, squeezing her tight, and whispered, "I knew you could do it." Meira then gave him and Haelyn a brief run-through of what had happened over the months she'd been gone. When she'd finally finished, Meira was uncertain that even her father believed it all—it was quite the yarn, she had to admit even to herself.

Haelyn took her aside after and told Meira how happy she was for her, and how relieved she was that she and Gaelen had returned safely. Meira was surprised at her cousin's words but thanked and gave her a hug.

Meira stood on the balcony of one of the castle chambers that Gaelen's servant had given her to ready for the ceremony, dressed in a soft blue gown that fell gracefully to her ankles with short, loose sleeves shaped like lilies of the valley. Her hair had been twisted and braided into a bun, leaving only a few loose curly strands to frame her face. The juniper tree pin from Gaelen had been fixed to the left side of her dress.

"Meira?" her father's voice called behind her.

Meira walked back into the room to find her father standing there with the door open. "You look lovely, Meira. Care to escort an old man to the ceremony?" he asked.

Meira smiled, joining her father and taking his arm. "Of course, Father," she said.

Meira and Lord Daesyn walked out of the chambers and down the hall at a leisurely pace, making their way toward the stairway so they could enter the throne room.

Noblemen and women stood on each side of the center aisle, waiting for the ceremony to start with varying degrees of patience. Meira and her father strode forward to take their places standing in front of two empty seats in the first row. She chewed on the inside of her lip nervously as she waited for the ceremony to start, wondering how Gaelen must be feeling.

Trumpeters entered from an entrance behind the throne's dais and began playing. The crowd hushed, waiting for Prince Gaelen to make his appearance. Gaelen stepped out onto the balcony above the dais, looking down at the crowd. He wore a blue cloak and a finely tailored shirt with the crest of Alythia embroidered on it. Meira watched him from below and smiled as they made eye contact before he descended.

Gaelen reached the bottom of the steps and strolled to the dais, where one of the council members stood waiting for him, holding a pillow with a golden crown sitting on it. He slowly walked up the steps of the dais, standing in front of the throne for a moment before taking a seat on his rightful throne. The council member walked to Gaelen's side, picking the crown up and gently placing it on his head before stepping back.

"Presenting his Royal Majesty, Gaelen Kyrell, King of Alythia."

* * *

Music reverberated through the ballroom once more as noblemen and women celebrated the crowning of their king. Meira danced in the center of the ballroom with Gaelen, laughing as he spun and twirled her. Noblemen and women standing off to the sides watched, clapping their hands in tune with the music.

The song ended, and Gaelen took Meira's hand, raising the back of it to his mouth to plant a kiss. Meira blushed, her heart still pounding in rhythm to the music as Gaelen leaned in close.

"Come on, there's something I want to show you," Gaelen whispered into her ear.

Meira let Gaelen lead her out of the ballroom and into the garden, walking down the steps. Gaelen pulled her hand as he started jogging toward the back of the garden. "Come on," he said.

Meira laughed, jogging behind him and keeping her hand in his. "Where are you taking me?"

"You'll see," he said with a playful chuckle.

Gaelen led her toward the back corner of the garden where the rundown tower stood. Meira cocked her head to one side curiously as they walked toward it, wondering why he'd taken her there. But then she looked up at the tower's window, where she saw it filled with a bright light.

Gaelen led Meira up the spiral staircase once more and pushed the door open. Meira entered, looking around the tower. Small balls of light flew along the ceiling, filling it up with light. Meira watched the balls and realized what they were—fairies. She gave Gaelen a curious look as he took her other hand and led her toward the window.

"Gaelen, what is this?" she asked.

Gaelen flashed her a grin, pulling her to the window and sitting on its ledge. Meira sat next to him, watching the fairies fly around the room. So many questions filled her head—why were the fairies here? Why had Gaelen brought her to the tower? Before she could think to ask her questions, Gaelen reached a hand up and brushed the side of her head with his hand, caressing her cheek.

"I love you, Meira Daesyn," he said, leaning in to kiss her.

Meira returned his kiss, her heart pounding in her chest as she realized what was happening. She reluctantly broke the kiss after a moment, pulling back to look up at him. "I love you too, Gaelen."

Gaelen reached his hand into his pants pocket, pulling out a small box and holding it out in front of her. Meira's eyes widened as she stared down at the box, her heart pounding fast in her chest.

"I've loved you since the day we met in the library all those years ago," Gaelen said, gazing at her as if she were his whole world. "You were my first real friend, and I missed you terribly in those years you spent away from the capital. Then you returned, and I resolved to have you as my wife, if you would have me as your husband. You saved my life and my kingdom, Meira. For that, you will always be honored in my court."

Meira flushed and smiled as she waited for him to go on. He hesitated only a few moments.

"Meira, I know you have doubts about being queen, but you are clever and brave and fiercely loyal to this land. I believe you will be the greatest queen in Alythia's history. So, I ask you again, will you marry me?"

Meira held her breath as he popped the box open and revealed the ring inside. It had a silver band set with a round, polished malachite gem, framed with tiny silver twigs of juniper on either side. Tears came to Meira's eyes as he took the ring out of the box.

"Yes, Gaelen. Yes!" she declared, beaming. She leaned in and kissed him heartily.

The kiss broke after a moment, and Gaelen took Meira's hand into his, sliding the silver band onto the ring finger of her left hand. He leaned his forehead against hers and smiled before standing and pulling her up with him, placing his hands on her waist. Unable to express his joy in words, Gaelen picked her up and began to spin, his smile bright and wide. Meira's laughter bubbled out of her as she was spun around and around. She put her arms around him as he put her back down and hugged him tight.

All around them, fairy lights flew, moving in between

their legs and circling their heads. Again Meira laughed, delighted as she watched the lights before looking back up at Gaelen and deep into his eyes. Once more she kissed him, savoring the moment all the more because she knew there would be many more like it in the years to come.

THE END

ABOUT THE AUTHOR

Ally (Allison) Kelly is a writer living in eastern Connecticut, USA, is owned by her orange cat, Merlin, and works part time in retail. Ally has been writing stories since she was young, and has grown fond of the fantasy genre over the years. She especially enjoys writing stories with dragons and fairies in them.

In 2016, Ally created an online writing community called Worldsmyths. Since then, the community has flourished. Worldsmyths Publishing, a non-profit indie publishing company, was established in 2021 to celebrate the five year anniversary of the community. Worldsmyths has since published multiple short story collections, a few of which Ally is published in.

Thorns Among Shadows is Ally's first official publication as an indie author, and her first fairytale retelling. She has

thoroughly enjoyed writing this book, and hopes to
continue with more retellings in the future!

Make sure to check out Ally's website and follow her on
social media!

http://akfantasywriter.com

facebook.com/AKFantasyWriter

instagram.com/AKFantasyWriter

tiktok.com/@authorallykelly

threads.net/@akfantasywriter

ACKNOWLEDGMENTS

There are so many people to acknowledge, I hardly know where to begin!

First, I'd like to thank my parents, sister and extended family. You've always been so encouraging and supportive of my dream to become an author, and I can't thank you enough for that.

To my best friend, Kira - writing is how we met! I can't imagine having gone through this publishing journey without you by my side! Thank you for being the best friend, Glinda to my Elphaba, and book event assistant I could ask for!

To my three favorite teachers, Mrs. Fontenault, Ms. Depew, and Mr. Stanizzi, without whom I wouldn't be the writer I am today.

To Freya Bell, C.P. Miller, and Odessa Silver - your friendship has come to mean *so* much to me since Worldsmyths first began, and I am incredibly thankful to all three of you for your never-ending encouragement and help throughout this whole process.

To the Worldsmyths community, who has been there through every step of the way to support me as I've worked toward publishing this book - I couldn't have done this without you all to push me into writing sprints and brain-storming sessions!

To Kyo, Tang, Penguin, and Irish, who all helped me get this book ready for the editor when crunch time came: THANK YOU!

To my editor, Nastasia of Stardust Book Services - thank you for your amazing feedback, and for helping me to whip this book into shape! If you are interested in Nastasia's editing services, you can visit her website at **www.stardust bookservices.com.**

Patron of the Arts Supporters

Siobahn Kinney

AUTHOR NEWSLETTER

Want to receive exclusive writing updates and publishing news? Subscribe to my newsletter!

BONUS SHORT STORY

The Drachenwald's Guardian is a short story, written by Ally
and published in the Worldsmyths short story anthology,
Myths, Legends & Dreams in 2021.

THE DRACHENWALD'S GUARDIAN
A SHORT STORY BY ALLY KELLY

Light filtered through the golden leaves and white branches of a tree onto Cathan's scales as he stood nearby on a cliff. His nostrils flared as he inhaled the heady smells of the forest below. He breathed in the smell of leaf mulch stirred by his clawed feet.

Cathan craned his long neck to observe the golden leaves of the Drachenwald tree, his green eyes glistening with a hint of matching gold. He snorted in satisfaction, lowering himself and tucking his front legs comfortably beneath his belly.

The forest was silent, just the way he liked it. No squirrels chattering as they collected their nuts, no birds twittering as they made their nests—they wouldn't dare! All the creatures of the forest knew who he was: Cathan, last of the dragons, guardian of the Drachenwald tree.

Cathan lowered his head toward the ground. A yawn revealed twin rows of long, sharp teeth and a forked serpentine tongue as he settled in for his afternoon nap. He closed his eyes, heaving a sigh.

An unfamiliar scent floating on the air caught his attention. He raised his head and looked around the edge of the clearing below, searching for an intruder—they were close. Very close. A low growl rose in his throat. How had he missed them until now? His shoulders rose in anger as he stood and stalked away from the tree, down into the clearing.

Cathan followed the scent to the lake's edge beneath his cliff, searching for the intruder. He stepped close to the water, his gaze sweeping the trees.

A twig snapped, and Cathan threw his body to his left, unfurling his wings. His ears pricked as he heard heavy breathing, and he lowered his head closer to one of the trees as he peered around it. The intruder gasped, flailing their arms as they fell. As they backed into a tree and pulled their legs to their chest, their hood fell to their shoulders.

A human girl.

Rage formed in the pit of his stomach. A human! Here, in his woods! He reared on his hind legs, extending his wings to their full length, and bellowed a thunderous roar that echoed through the valley and shook the ground beneath his feet.

How dare a human come here, near the last Drachen-wald tree, after the others were destroyed? Did she not know the story? Cathan studied her face as she raised her hands over her ears, covering them with her palms beneath messy, curly brown hair. Two green eyes surrounded by a rounded face gazed up at him and Cathan snapped his jaw shut as his roar faded, then he lowered his head to look down at the girl.

Part of him wanted to strike out at her right then—humans had invaded his home, hunted down the other dragons, and destroyed the other Drachenwald trees, leaving only one behind. Though he had gotten used to his life of solitude, the ache in his heart for his fellow dragons had never faded.

As he watched the girl shaking like a leaf on the ground in front of him, the voice of Cathan's empathy spoke out. *She's just a girl,* he thought. *She has nothing to do with the actions of other humans.* She couldn't be more than sixteen years old judging from her size and scent, and the other dragons had been gone for decades. Despite his feelings toward humans, killing her seemed distasteful.

Cathan huffed, baring his teeth, his nostrils flaring. "Who are you, and what are you doing in my forest?"

The girl raised her head, staring up at him with wide eyes. She started to speak, but could barely form the words as they caught in her throat.

Cathan bared his teeth again, growing impatient. "Tell me your name!" he growled.

"Niamh. Please, don't eat me," she begged, her voice shaking.

Cathan's cold laughter echoed throughout the clearing. "Child, if I wanted to eat you, I'd have done it within seconds of seeing you. Now, what are you doing in my forest?"

"My sister has been taken by slavers. I need help finding them and getting her back," she answered in a trembling voice. "I was following them and found my way here, but I tripped and hurt my ankle,"

Cathan raised his head. Did that mean there were others in the forest looming closer to the tree? "Come closer. I will not hurt you," he said.

He waited for the girl to obey. The fear fell from her face, replaced by curiosity, as she leaned forward from the tree. "You really are a dragon, aren't you?"

"My name is Cathan. I am the guardian of this forest, and you are trespassing," he growled.

Niamh stared up at him in awe. "I've never seen a dragon before. I was always told they'd all been hunted down. Some said they weren't real."

Cathan lowered his head toward her. "I assure you, I am quite real. See for yourself."

Niamh hesitantly raised her hand toward him. Her fingers hesitated for a moment before she finally touched the end of his snout near his nostrils, running her hand over his rough, warm scales.

Cathan closed his eyes, breathing in her scent as Niamh's fingers touched him. His snout twitched, and her earthy human scent filled his nostrils as he tried to sniff out the scents of the slavers. There was something else, something faint but familiar. He shut his eyes tighter, trying to remember. He'd smelled something similar a long time ago, but recognition eluded him. Abandoning the effort, he lifted his lids and watched Niamh's eyes fill with even more curiosity. They held an interesting mix of innocence and sorrow.

"I never expected to talk to a dragon," Niamh said, lowering her hand.

Cathan watched the girl, contemplating his response as he pulled his head back. He didn't want to stray too far from the tree, and who knew where these slavers were by now?

"Do you know where these slavers were going?" he asked.

"Toward Rhothia," Niamh replied.

Cathan studied her skeptically as he considered her story. The city of Rhothia was much further outside the border of the forest than Cathan would have liked. Nearly a half day's walk for a human. He didn't like the idea of her kind being here, and the sooner they left, the better. He couldn't risk leaving the tree unguarded for long, though.

It won't happen again. Not under my watch, he thought, remembering the beautiful leaves of the other Drachenwald trees burning before shaking off the painful memory. He had to get Niamh as far away from the tree as he could.

Staying in this form would make the journey difficult, however. Riding was a special privilege reserved for those bonded to a dragon. Besides, it would be easier to pass through the trees and keep a closer eye on her if he wasn't in this form.

Cathan huffed and rose from the ground. "I will help you. But first, I must take care of something. Stay here," he said.

He entered the shallow lake and walked toward the cave behind the waterfall. As he entered the cave's darkness, his shifting magic stirred within him, clawing at his insides. A long growl escaped him, echoing throughout the cave as it continued ripping at him. Bones crunched and flesh squelched as his body shifted. Wings shrank into his back and disappeared. His claws did the same, forming human hands and feet, and his limbs shortened into arms and legs.

He fumbled in the darkness as his eyes struggled to adjust, and he searched for the pile of human clothing made in the nation of Elisora he kept for when he shifted to this form—not that he shifted very often. He detested being in his human form.

Niamh's jaw dropped as he approached after emerging from the cave. "You can shift into a human?"

Cathan glanced down at himself and considered what he looked like to her. He wore a long-sleeved tunic, simple pants and boots, and a cloak wrapped tight with the hood drawn down, revealing a short beard and sharp jaw, and a head of brown hair that was shorn close to his scalp.

"I assure you that dragons are capable of far more than simply burning down villages, or whatever your fellow humans would have told you," Cathan answered with a shrug. "Now, come along. The sooner we find your sister, the sooner I can return home." He jumped from the last rock onto the beach, then walked toward Niamh. "Can you put any weight on your foot?"

Niamh stood straight against the tree and placed her foot on the ground. She winced and shifted her weight off of it. "Some, but it'll slow me down."

Cathan sighed. This would take longer than he'd hoped. He searched for a sturdy branch, found one that satisfied him, then offered it to her. "Here, use this as a walking stick." He grabbed the crook of Niamh's arm, staring her hard in the eyes. "If we pass anyone, say nothing about who I am if they ask. Understood?" Cathan kept his voice low.

Niamh silently nodded, waiting for him to let her go. Cathan watched her for a moment before he turned back toward the Drachenwald tree. Its leaves contained protective magic that could prove useful on this journey. He considered returning to the tree to collect a few, then dismissed the notion with a confident shrug as he turned back.

They traveled until it became too dark to see and made camp for the night.

* * *

Early the next morning, Cathan watched as the clouds drifted along the morning sky, and yearned to be up there with them, gliding along with his wings spread wide as he searched for the intruders. He heaved a frustrated sigh, his body visibly shuddering. How long had it been since they'd left the Drachenwald tree? Not long by his calculation. *I'll never get used to being in this body,* he thought.

"Are you alright?" Niamh asked nervously.

Cathan glanced over at Niamh and nodded as they walked up the crest of a hill. "I'm just eager to get back home." His transformation magic stirred within him, but it felt off. "I think there's a shortcut we can take through the woods over there that will lead toward Rhothia," Cathan said, pointing toward the woods up ahead.

"Are you sure that's the right way?" Niamh asked.

Cathan frowned. His senses weren't as sharp in his human form as they were in his dragon one—his vision became blurry if he tried to see too far away, and he couldn't hear the whir of a cricket's wings from across the clearing like he could as a dragon. His sense of smell may as well have been non-existent. But he still had a good sense of direction. He glanced over at Niamh, trying to read her face.

"I'm sure. This will be faster," Cathan replied.

Niamh limped ahead of him as they came to the wooded entrance, sitting down on a nearby log. Her breathing was heavy as she leaned forward, grasping her ankle. "I can't walk anymore. My ankle's getting worse."

Cathan sighed in frustration. *I should just leave her here,* he thought, but they were still too close to the Drachenwald. He looked at Niamh as she sat on the log, watching as she rubbed at her ankle. How hard it must have been for humans to be unable to heal their injuries with magic. His empathy overcame his draconic instincts once more as he realized how weak she truly was, and he felt a strange sense of caring for the girl. He chewed on the inside of his lip as he knelt down in front of her. "Let me see," he said.

Niamh raised the edge of her skirts, allowing him to examine her ankle. Cathan lifted her leg up, so it rested on his knee and he could examine it. "It's a little swollen, but not too bad," he said. He pulled a strip of his cloak off and carefully wrapped it around her ankle.

Niamh used the branch to stand, trying to maintain balance on one foot. "Thank you," she said.

As they walked further, he opened and closed his fists anxiously. He was too far from home, and she was walking slow enough that he'd never make it back before sunrise the next day.

"Is there any chance we can stop? I'm getting tired," Niamh pleaded from his side.

Cathan shook his head. "We have to keep going. I want to get as far as possible today."

Silence lingered between them once more. Cathan noticed Niamh glancing up at him before quickly looking away.

"What is it?" he asked.

Niamh bit her lip. "Why do you not want humans in the forest?"

"Have you not heard the stories of what happened between the humans and dragons?" Cathan asked, surprised. Didn't most humans know the story by now?

Niamh shrugged. "I know there used to be lots of drag-ons, but not what happened to them."

Cathan took a deep breath as he began."The humans and dragons had a pact to protect the Drachenwald trees. Some humans held magical connections to dragons, though it was rare. One such human existed and held a connection with a dragon. The human promised to train and become a guardian of the Drachenwald trees, keeping them protected from those who sought to use their magic for other means. Some humans hunted the dragons down to sell their parts at markets." He breathed deeply, keeping his gaze forward as they walked. "The human and dragon shared everything, even emotions, which made the betrayal even more bitter when he betrayed his dragon and led a massacre to the forest. The humans destroyed all but one Drachenwald tree. One tree, and one dragon as its guardian, are all that remain."

"How is it you survived?" Niamh asked, wincing.

Cathan glanced down at his side, feeling a phantom pain from the nearly fatal stab wound he'd endured all those years ago. "I almost didn't," he answered. "The rest of my kind were not so lucky . . ."

He trailed. "The humans had torn the power from the Drachenwald trees and turned against their partners." He pushed the thoughts out of his mind, wishing he could claw them away permanently. Now the responsibility of protecting the tree had fallen to him, and although he'd accepted it willingly, it was a heavy burden to bear on his own. He felt the familiar urge to shed a tear, but ignored it.

"I'm sorry," Niamh said. She wiped a tear away and looked down at her damp fingers in surprise.

"It was a long time ago," Cathan replied. "I prefer not to dwell on it."

"Why did you decide to help me?" Niamh asked.

Cathan kept his gaze straight ahead. "The sooner you're out of the forest, the sooner I can get back home." As he walked, he listened for the sound of her feet moving through the grass. "I can easily turn back, so you better keep up if you expect me to help you find your sister," he called back to her.

Niamh appeared at his side a few moments later as she limped quickly to catch up.

"Have you ever been to Rhothia?" Niamh asked.

"Only once, many years ago," Cathan answered after a moment.

Rhothia sat outside the capital of Valena as a merchant city. Many tradespeople from all over came to the city to sell their treasures—including the hunters that had murdered so many of his kind. Dragons were drawn to treasure, especially young ones, and Cathan had been no exception. His curiosity had allowed him to take advantage of his shifting magic and enter the city as though he were any other human.

He had wandered the streets, taking in the exotic wares from lands he had never traveled to himself. But his awe had turned to horror, then rage, when he caught sight of a dragon skull, on a merchant's table with a handful of dragon scales, glistening in the scorching sun. His stomach churned, unable to keep himself from imagining what those dragons must have endured for humans to have their expensive trinkets.

Cathan shook the memory away and looked to Niamh, who stared up at him with confusion. He cleared his throat, looking away. "I went there once to explore the city. Let's just say I didn't like what I saw."

Niamh nodded. "I was born in Rhothia. I remember wandering the markets and seeing . . ."

"Seeing what?" Cathan asked.

Niamh paused and looked up at him, sorrow in her voice. "The magical creatures some of the merchants had in cages."

As Cathan held eye contact with Niamh, a warm prickling filled his stomach as his magic stirred—not the way it did when he was about to transform, but when his magic reacted to danger. He scowled, tilting his head to one side as he tried to make sense of it.

"We should keep going," Niamh said, pulling her gaze away. "You need to get back to your tree, after all."

* * *

A few hours later, Cathan followed the path in the forest, stepping over a large branch jutting up from the forest floor. The path ended in a clearing with leaves covering the ground, and he walked further in.

Something stirred on the ground. Before Cathan could react, a net flew up around him, knocking him off his feet as it rose swiftly into the air. Cathan snarled and thrashed at the ropes, his draconian instincts surging to the fore. His eyes dilating, his tongue darted out of his mouth and he bit at the net with his dull human teeth. His clawless fingers tore at the ropes, and his shoulder blades twitched with the urge to take flight.

Above, six humans sat up in the trees, three on each side of the clearing as they held the ropes and pulled the net further into the air.

Damn humans, he thought angrily. *I should have known better.*

If only he were in his dragon form—he'd rip them apart and burn them to a crisp in a matter of seconds! He pulled on his shifting magic, hoping he could transform and free himself, but the magic was weak.

Come on, he begged inwardly. *Don't fail me now!*

He tried again, continuing to thrash and snarl as he attempted to free himself, but it was no use. The powerful magic he'd always known within him was too weak for a full transformation. He was too far from the tree.

Consider yourselves lucky, he thought.

A man with a dark beard peppered with grey approached the net, coming up to Cathan's chest. He peered up at him, and Cathan gave him a hard glare as he held onto the net.

"What do you want?" Cathan demanded, his voice rumbling.

The man grinned. "Rumor in Rhothia has it that the townspeople have seen the shadow of a dragon flying over this forest, but no one was brave enough to find out if it was true. From what I know of dragonlore, some have shapeshifting abilities." He paused, tossing his head back in Niamh's direction. "Your little friend here confirmed who you were."

Cathan looked behind the man to where Niamh struggled beneath another net as two men clutched her arms tight. The human standing in front of Cathan's net turned toward Niamh and approached, pulling the net off of her and keeping his back turned, making it harder for Cathan to hear what he said to her.

The man turned away. "Cut him down and tie him up. We'll make camp here for the night before we head to Rhothia."

The net holding Cathan fell from the air and onto the ground with Cathan in it, knocking the air out of him as he landed on his stomach. Hands grabbed at his arms from both sides and yanked him up as Niamh, free from her net, walked toward him. He met her gaze.

"You don't have a sister, do you?" Niamh didn't answer. "Tell me, how does it feel to betray a dragon?" He held eye contact with the human girl, searching her eyes as a ghostly twinge of guilt tugged at his gut.

"I had no choice." Her voice was soft as she turned away.

* * *

Cathan pulled against the thick, glittering chains wrapped tight around his chest as he sat against the trunk of a tree while the humans set camp, but it was no use. Sweat drenched his forehead, and he hung his head low, growling in frustration. He couldn't shift, and he didn't have enough strength to rip through the chains holding him against the tree.

He closed his eyes, fighting to control his breathing. He would never escape from these humans if he wasted what remained of his strength. Strands of hair fell into his face, and he shook them away to see where Niamh sat with her companions around a campfire.

"Go bring him some water. We can't have him dying on us before we reach Rhothia," one of the male humans said, cuffing Niamh on the head.

Cathan raised an eyebrow as she turned toward him with a scowl, making eye contact. Niamh stood in front of him a few moments later. She knelt down and held a cup toward him. "I'm sorry they've been so cruel to you," Niamh said, keeping her voice low. "Gavriel takes too much pleasure in tormenting others."

Cathan glanced skeptically at the cup, but nodded and allowed Niamh to raise it to his lips. "Thank you," Cathan said as he pulled back. "Is Gavriel the leader?" She nodded. "Tell me, how much are they paying you to help them?"

Niamh gazed up at him, a hint of defiance in her eyes, but Cathan could see the truth in them. He watched as she absently rubbed at the iron cuff on her left wrist, and Cathan understood even more. He'd seen such iron cuffs before, many years ago when he'd visited Rhothia, on the wrist of the merchant with the dragon skull on display. She needed help as much as he did.

"You don't have to do this," Cathan said, keeping his voice soft. He watched the other humans sitting several feet away from them as they talked. "I know you're a good person, and we can help each other."

Niamh stayed silent.

"If you help me escape from here, we can go to the Drachenwald tree, and I will make sure these men can never find you." He paused, letting that information sink in before continuing. "I am the tree's guardian. My shifting magic is tied to the tree's. But the longer I stay here, in this form, the more vulnerable the tree is. I need to get back to it. Will you help me?"

"Niamh! Come back over here!"

Niamh raised her eyes to him and stood, then walked away silently. Cathan watched as Niamh lay down on her bedroll, her shoulders hunched. Cathan could tell she was having a hard time getting comfortable as she constantly shifted her body. He hoped she would roll over so they could continue their wordless conversation, but she never did.

* * *

Cathan was woken early the next morning. Gavriel stood nearby and watched as his men restrained Cathan with the chains that had held him to the tree all night. Once he was secure, Gavriel pulled him forward with a sharp tug. Cathan struggled against it, but Gavriel just laughed. "That chain binds you with magic. You'll only escape it when I release you from it, and you'll stay human until I say so." He fondled a heavy gold key on a thong around his neck.

"Where are you taking me?" Cathan asked.

"To the marketplace in Rhothia," Gavriel answered.

"Good luck with that," Cathan scoffed as he watched Gavriel's reaction.

Gavriel raised an eyebrow. "Why is that?"

Cathan looked instinctively in the direction of the Drachenwald, barely able to sense its power. He needed to be closer to break free, but the thought of these humans taking one step nearer terrified him. Niamh gasped.

Gavriel turned toward Niamh, who stood nearby. "Do you know why?"

Niamh looked away, not meeting his eyes. Gavriel grabbed her by the arm, shaking her. She bit her lip and gave Cathan an agonized look. "The tree," she whispered.

Gavriel raised his fist, and she cowered with familiar fear. "What tree?" he asked.

Cathan's eyes widened, and he snarled at Niamh. "Say nothing."

Gavriel laughed. "She knows who she belongs to."

Niamh bowed her head and pointed in the tree's direction. "It has great power."

Gaviel's mouth widened in a vicious smile. "Great power, you say?" He turned toward one of his lackeys. "Break camp. We have a new destination."

Cathan struggled against his chains with futile desperation.

* * *

After hours of traveling, Cathan sat up against the trunk of a tree that night, chains tied tight around his chest. He eyed Niamh suspiciously as she approached him.

Niamh knelt down next to him, holding a golden key in her hand as she fumbled with the chain's lock. "We have little time. Gavriel is keeping watch and is stinking drunk," Niamh whispered.

"Is that how you got the key?" Cathan asked.

Niamh nodded. "I took it off of him after he passed out. He's not very good at keeping watch."

"Clearly, but how do I know this isn't another trap?"

"You don't. You'll just have to trust me. Hold the chains tight so they don't fall when I unlock them. If we make too much noise Gavriel might wake up."

Cathan nodded, watching as she twisted the key into the lock. "What changed your mind?"

The lock turned with a click and Niamh began to slowly remove the chains. "I've helped Gavriel hurt too many magical creatures already. I don't know why, but I couldn't let him hurt you."

"Why did the hunters have you with them?" Cathan inquired.

"I'm the bait," Niamh answered. "They travel all over the country, collecting magical items and creatures to sell. Gavriel kidnapped me with this cuff and forced me to work with them, since I don't look like a hunter. He uses me as a decoy to lure magical creatures—like you." She raised her left wrist to show him the iron cuff.

"Are you sure you want to do this? There's no going back."

"I'm sure," Niamh answered. "Are you able to transform yet?"

As the last loop of chain was quietly set on the ground, Cathan stood. His legs and arms felt cramped from sitting for so long, but he was free. His magic stirred within him, but returning to his true form took far more energy than shedding it. He turned toward Niamh and shook his head. "Not yet. We're getting closer. Let's go."

* * *

Cathan pushed himself to walk as fast as he could, with Niamh barely trailing behind. As they came closer to the Drachenwald tree, he could feel his power growing. The morning sun had begun its rise over the treetops in the distance.

Soon, he thought. He could return to his true form and fulfill his promise — not just to protect the Drachenwald tree, but to protect Niamh as well.

He reached up toward the clasp of his cloak, pulling it open and letting it drop to the ground. He held his gaze steady, walking faster as his transformation magic stirred within him. Clothes tore from his body as he grew, his legs and arms changing shape. Claws replaced fingers and toes, and two wings grew out of his shoulder blades. His long neck stretched toward the sky, and his jaw opened to reveal twin rows of dagger-like teeth.

Cathan felt an echo of both tension and excitement. He lowered his head, pausing it only inches from Niamh's face as he stared into her eyes.

"You've granted me my freedom. What would you ask of me in return?"

Niamh swallowed, the fear in her eyes fading into determination. "I want Gavriel to get what he deserves."

"Something we have in common," Cathan said. "What do you plan to do afterwards, when you've gained your freedom from these men?"

Niamh's eyes widened as she considered the question and looked away. She shook her head. "I'm not sure. I have no family or home left to go to."

Cathan nodded, looking out into the distance, to where he could imagine the golden treetop of the Drachenwald, glistening in the sunlight. He raised his head toward the sky and closed his eyes, breathing in. Soon, he could put everything that had happened behind him and go back to protecting the tree. *Perhaps I won't be doing it alone, though,* he thought as he opened his eyes.

As Cathan came up the crest of the hill, a familiar woodsy scent entered his nostrils and he paused, baring his teeth as rage filled his belly. Gavriel led his caravan toward the bottom of the cliff, pointing toward the tree as he and his men shouted their cheers of victory.

"Stay here." Cathan's wings spread out next to him and he took off into the air, leaving Niamh behind on the hillside.

Cathan flew high above the caravan, watching as Gavriel's lackeys stood paralyzed in fear. He searched for Gavriel, whose horse was already beginning the climb up the cliff toward the tree. Cathan's roar echoed throughout the valley, and he dove toward the cliff, landing in front of Gavriel's horse as he spread his wings out to their full length. Gavriel stared up at him in horror, his hand shaking as he raised his sword in a feeble attempt to protect himself.

Cathan growled, baring his teeth and lowering his head

as close to Gavriel's face as he could. "I told you I'd rip you limb from limb." He opened his mouth, feeling the rage build up in his belly as foam slipped through his teeth and dripped onto his chin.

"Wait!" Gavriel exclaimed, dropping the sword as he held up one hand. "I can offer you riches or anything else you want! Look, I'll prove it!" He reached slowly into a pouch he wore on his belt, pulling out a pile of dragon scales and dropping them to the ground.

Cathan reared back on his legs, shaking his head in a fiery rage. The ground beneath him shook as he roared, sending more of Gavriel's men scattering away. Gavriel's horse followed, leaving its owner behind. "This is your idea of a bribe? Throwing the scales of my brethren at my feet?" he scoffed. "You lost your life when you captured me."

For a moment, Cathan forgot about Niamh, about the other men, focusing on Gavriel instead. It was because of greedy men like Gavriel that the other dragons had been killed, and now the results lay in front of him. It would be Gavriel's last mistake.

Out of the corner of one eye, he saw Niamh approach, and he raised his head. His eyes flickered toward her, watching as she carefully approached Gavriel.

Gavriel turned toward Niamh. "You think this dragon will do a better job than me taking care of you? I put food in your belly. How can you trust him not to eat you?"

Niamh looked up at Cathan, who raised his chin in acknowledgement. As they made eye contact, he felt a sense of kinship coming from her.

"I trust him more than I ever trusted you," she said after a moment, looking back at Gavriel. "You took me from the only home I ever knew and used me for your own personal gain." She looked up at Cathan, who waited patiently for her signal as he sensed the rage radiating off of her, and she stared down at her former captor. "You may have put food in my belly, but you *never* took care of me," she said as her breathing slowed.

"You'll never get by on your own without me, girl," Gavriel scoffed.

Niamh reached toward the chain hanging around Gavriel's neck and yanked it off. She held the silver key in her palm before looking back at him. "I'm done doing your dirty work."

Niamh raised her left wrist, clicking the key into the lock and holding it there for a moment before letting the iron cuff fall to the ground in front of Gavriel.

Gavriel stared down at the cuff before looking back between Niamh and Cathan, his eyes wide with fear.

Niamh turned away from Gavriel and looked up at Cathan, who nodded, waiting for her to move.

A blood-curdling scream echoed throughout the valley.

* * *

After taking care of Gavriel's lackeys, Cathan looked toward the cliff where the Drachenwald tree stood, closing his eyes as the tree's magic wrapped itself around him, welcoming him back.

Cathan turned toward Niamh, who knelt on the ground several feet away. His magic stirred, and he sensed her confusion, relief, and uncertainty radiating off of her. Part of him wanted to ignore it and let her go her own way, but the magic was strong. It had been many years since the last dragon bonded with a human, but Cathan couldn't deny the familiar feeling of a bond forming any longer.

"Are you alright?" he asked as he walked toward her.

Niamh looked up at him, tears streaming down her face. "I've wanted to escape from Gavriel for so long, and I couldn't . . . until now. You gave me that strength, Cathan."

Cathan shook his head. "You've always had that strength within you. In time, you'll learn to use it for things you can't imagine," he said.

Niamh frowned, wiping her tears away as she stood. "What do you mean?"

"Come with me, and I'll show you."

Cathan led her forward, pausing near the base of the tree, gazing on its golden leaves glistening in the beaming sun.

Niamh paused at his side, her mouth gaped open in awe.

"Did I not tell you the tree was magnificent?" Cathan asked.

"It's the most beautiful tree I've ever seen," Niamh whispered in awe.

"Being a guardian of this tree is not something to take lightly," he said. "A guardian is forever bound, not just with physically protecting it, but because of the magical connection a guardian has to the tree. It is a lifelong commitment." He lowered his head in front of her. "You said before that you don't have a place to call home. You can stay here and learn more about the tree. If it goes well, this may become a permanent home for you."

Niamh's green eyes widened, and she smiled up at him. "You'd really allow me to stay here?"

Cathan nodded. "For as long as you'd like."

"I don't know what to say . . . thank you, Cathan."

"We have much to learn from each other, I think," Cathan said, looking up at the tree. For the first time in many years, a weight had lifted from his shoulders. Finally, he would have someone to share his duties with, and he could take to the sky more often. He wouldn't be alone anymore. He looked down at Niamh again, lowering his neck. "If you're going to live here, you should see your new home from above."

PUBLICATIONS

Check out these short story collections that Ally has been published in, all available on Amazon!

Myths, Legends & Dreams: A Worldsmyths Anthology

Darkness & Moonlight: A Worldsmyths Anthology

Written in the Wind: A Worldsmyths Anthology

WORLDSMYTHS WRITING COMMUNITY

Worldsmyths is a writing community for speculative fiction writers. Originally established in 2014 as a forum, Worldsmyths has grown into a Discord community with over 900 members.

Want to be a part of this amazing community? Visit the Worldsmyths website at http://worldsmyths.com or join our Discord community here https://discord.gg/kT27Uk FAEU

www.ingramcontent.com/pod-product-compliance
Lightning Source LLC
Chambersburg PA
CBHW070357200726

48294CB00003B/961